THE HOPLI~~~

THE HOPLINESS OF LIFE

Short Stories

Anne Armitage

© Anne Armitage, 2021

Published by Coppice Books

bookscoppice@gmail.com

A CIP catalogue record for this book is available from the British Library.

ISBN 978-1-9989915-1-8

Book layout and cover design by Clare Brayshaw

Cover image © Berkay | Dreamstime.com

Prepared and printed by:

York Publishing Services Ltd
64 Hallfield Road
Layerthorpe
York YO31 7ZQ

Tel: 01904 431213

Website: www.yps-publishing.co.uk

For my granddaughter, Lily,

who invented the concept of Hopliness

Contents

Author's Note

WHEN my granddaughter, Lily, was about four years old, I was out walking with her and my son and some of their friends. Among the group was a younger child about three, whom Lily was eager to impress with her 'grown-upness' and her knowledge. So she plucked a piece of sedge grass and as she pointed to the way that the stem changed colour as you looked along it, she said to the other girl, "You see that there, the way it's one colour there and then down there it's a different colour? Well, that's its 'hopliness'." There was hardly a pause in the sentence as her mind raced to find the word that would fit what she was trying to express. There wasn't one, so she invented one and her delivery was seamless. I was very impressed and I really do think that such a word should be in the dictionary, for it perfectly describes that very 'itness' of things.

Life is full of entanglements, of deep-rooted loves and hates, of kindnesses and cruelty. I have, therefore, used the word 'hopliness' to describe this collection of short stories, which deal with those brief and singular moments in life that remain with one forever. They also explore the vagaries of human behaviour, both comic and tragic, and examine the good and evil that people are capable of and, indeed, all the stages in between.

Anne Armitage

One-woman Crusade

THE lane up to the waterfalls, a famed local beauty spot, went past Sarah's house. This was a double-fronted stone cottage in a row of six just on the edge of a small village in which all the houses were built in the same local stone. The village was deemed by many a guide book to be picturesque. Indeed, it drew crowds all year round. Some came just to enjoy the village atmosphere, to eat and drink in the local pub or, in the summer, to let the kids paddle in the stream. The more adventurous liked to walk the four miles up the road to the spectacular falls.

Sarah had never married. Indeed, she had never felt the need to. She remembered going to a wedding when she was about fourteen and someone had asked an aged aunt why she had never married and her reply was, "I've never been kissed, kicked or run over." Sarah noticed that this was said with some pride. And so it was for Sarah. She had experienced neither the excitement nor the upheaval of the married state and had lived contentedly in the cottage all her life, inheriting it when her parents died. Her father had been an English teacher at the nearby grammar school and her mother the district nurse. Sarah had been the local primary school teacher and so knew nearly everyone in the village, except for the incomers with second homes. It was a matter of pride to her to keep her frontage in bloom all year long so that it would give pleasure to the passers-by and sometimes earn gratifying praise from them. It was also instrumental in helping the village to claim the 'Best Kept Village' award, year after year.

However, lately, Sarah had developed an obsession with dogs. Well, not exactly dogs, but dog shit. She had become tired and infuriated by the number of times in the past year that she had stepped into a pile of it just by her front door. Then she had to clean up the flags outside and, of course, her shoes. It was revolting and had to stop. So, she put up notices in both front windows, then one on her front door and one on the lamp post opposite her cottage requesting, even begging, dog owners to be more considerate. She even put a poop scoop and some plastic bags in a convenient, but prominent place, as a further hint to dog owners to take home their mess. It hadn't made any difference.

In order to try and do something more about all this, she positioned an armchair in the front window, behind the net curtain, so that she could see walkers approaching up the lane and would be ready to spring into action if their dog looked like slowing down outside her property. In fact, she was sitting there one day last year when a young man came up the lane with two dogs, little Skye terriers; one on the lead and the other under his arm. He was of small build, with dark curly hair and heavy-rimmed glasses and looked a bit, what her mother might have called, 'precious'. The dog on the lead slowed down and Sarah was off like a whippet out of a trap. She flung open the front door and was about to let rip, when the young man said, "Oh, I am sorry. I was just admiring your roses. I didn't mean to disturb you. They are beautiful. You should be very proud of your display."

Well, she was quite taken aback for a moment and then thought that she must return the compliment by praising his dogs, so she said, "What lovely little dogs you have there. Are they well behaved? What do you call them?"

"This one," he said, pointing to the one under his arm, "is Gerard Manley Hopkins and the other is Percy Bysshe Shelley."

"That's grand," she said. "What interesting names."

You could have knocked her down with a feather. How did he call them back when they were off the lead? That would certainly lead to some comments. Honestly, what would people think of next?

However, she had begun to think a lot about dogs' names of late because she couldn't believe how many dogs people had now and what barmy names they were calling them. Archie, Charlie and Max seemed to be popular calls out in the lane and Sarah couldn't be sure whether they were shouting to the children or the dogs. But that was all right because there was still a link to the real world in those names. But nowadays there were more Diesels, Bandits and Mooses going past, not to mention Bears, Bentleys, Winstons and, one step too far for Sarah, Zeus and Apollo. She had heard them all called out at least once from the comfort of her armchair behind the net curtain. The female dogs' names were also going slightly off the scale with Nalas, Lunas, Novas and even Athena; she had heard that called out only yesterday. "What planet do these people inhabit?" she thought. "Disney probably." To Sarah, it seemed that there must be more dogs than humans in the world nowadays. People didn't seem to be happy with only one. They now had to have two or three per household. "We will be overrun soon," she often thought, "and what about the vets' bills? Do they think of that before they buy?" She was sure that there would be lots of stray dogs around in the future when the cost got too much. People were just following fashion. She had also noticed lately how many TV adverts included a dog in their sales pitch and you couldn't move in the local pub for dogs. That never used to be allowed. Something should be done about it. It was unhygienic.

When Sarah was young, most of the dogs in the village were working or hunting dogs. In fact, the local hunt passed through the village several times a year and there were often shooting parties on the local grand estate. She didn't object to those kinds of dogs. And, of course, some people kept a pet for companionship, like the old lady two doors down, who had a corgi because the Queen liked corgis, and that was okay. In fact, most dogs around when she was a child were mongrels and there wasn't this craze for dogs like there was today. She was absolutely shocked recently when she learned what people were paying for such puppies. Thousands of pounds. The other day she had seen a young girl, whom she knew in the village, with a new puppy of the fad variety and she could not believe that her family had that kind of money to throw around. It must be the pester factor, like those tempting sweets at the supermarket checkout. Sometimes, lately, on village fête days, Sarah had seen grown men, who wouldn't be caught hugging their sons, cuddling little balls of fluff like besotted lovers and she knew, without a shadow of doubt, that those men had not chosen that toy, but had fallen in love with it nevertheless. Where would it end? The world had gone mad.

On her Facebook account, Sarah liked to keep up with what her cousins' children were doing and had become intrigued by the number of posts about dog-snatching. She wasn't at all surprised. With so much money changing hands in the dog-fad market, it was bound to happen. If you were daft enough to shell out £2000 for a puppy, then some savvy criminal was bound to want to get his hands on it, either to sell it on for a profit or breed from it. What a world we have made! She also noticed, while scrolling through her Facebook posts, how women, in particular, swooned over pictures of friends' new puppies. It was almost as if they had had a new baby and, of course, in many ways they had. But, how sad was that? Surely, they could have another baby, learn to love another human being, if they felt that way? After a few years, you wouldn't have to carry plastic bags around to pick up the mess and it would learn to feed itself eventually. The same gang of coo-ers were also only too eager, in dog solidarity, to post alarm calls when someone's beloved dog went missing; presumably, these days, snatched, even if the distraught person was a complete stranger. And, it was no surprise to Sarah, on seeing the photos of these darling pooches, that they were nearly all what she called fad dogs; the absolute 'must-haves'. Somehow, it reminded her of the dog-catcher part of *The Lady and the Tramp*. Fortunately that was only fiction so one could dismiss it. However, she could not ignore the fever that had apparently taken over society with regard to dogs.

Sarah had become interested in studying the people coming up the lane and liked to match them with the breed of dog they had chosen. She was convinced that you could gauge how intelligent the owners were by the dog they had. What did a little white fluffy thing with appealing eyes say about you? She knew what she thought. It would make a good social science project for some eager student. Almost everyone coming by, without exception, seemed to exude a sense of entitlement in their dog ownership. If she was out in village or the countryside, she had noticed of late that people with dogs made a fuss of their dog as they approached you and looked up at you as they passed with an almost sanctified air - the chosen ones. You were required to say something nice about their pooch and, if you ignored it, you were somehow made to feel churlish and grumpy; unsociable even. When did we need dogs to get into conversation with strangers? Sarah had never needed one. She liked real conversation about real things, not about someone's pet. It was so shallow. But then the young, with all their gadgets, had forgotten how to make conversation, so perhaps the dogs were necessary for the survival of human interaction.

In her study of the dog-owning fraternity, Sarah had mentally divided them into groups:-

Group A – The Real People

These were the owners who had chosen what Sarah called 'real' dogs; old breeds, dogs that weren't showy, sound, reliable dogs like collies, retrievers, labradors and spaniels. They just wanted a dog, preferably one that spoke of country pursuits, to make their family complete. These people weren't out to impress, or so the owners pleaded, but such dogs did tend to be a very aspiring, middle-class choice, or so Sarah felt.

Group B – The Big Dog People

People who owned such dogs wanted hair and bigness and lovable floppiness. This group chose dogs like St Bernards, Pyrenean mountain dogs and Newfoundlands and she had noticed that such owners came to the village in large camper vans. They would have to, looking at the size of their hounds. With these people, the dog was their life's mission. "Good luck to them," Sarah often thought when they passed by. "God knows what their carpets are like."

Group C – The Man's Dog

These dogs were usually chosen by men who wanted to demonstrate strength in some way, either in the dog's build or its aggressive character. Favourite breeds seemed to be Rottweilers, Boxer dogs, Dobermans, mastiffs and bulldogs. Scary dogs meant to intimidate. Too much testosterone on show for her liking.

Group D – The Woman's Dog

Little terriers of all kinds. Pugs, Springer spaniels and, top of the list, the cockapoo and the labradoodle. These names were meant to suggest cuddliness, but really it was genetic meddling which she felt would end in tears, for the dogs that is. Oh, and one must not forget the 'shit-soos', or whatever they were called; quite an appropriate name though, you had to admit. At this point, Sarah gave up. There were so many 'adorable' dogs being bred that she hoped that the God of Dogs would intervene, sooner or later, and stop this madness.

Group E – The Toy Dogs

With regard to this group, Sarah could not speak without getting overheated. Dogs being bred toy-size for people to play with. Shameful. She had once seen a couple out with a Chihuahua on whose feet the woman had put little leather boots. When the dog jumped off the low wall, where she was displaying this 'cute' little performer, she just yanked it back up by its lead. They should be shot. Not the dogs, the owners.

Sometimes, Sarah found that she had placed someone in the wrong dog-owner category and this intrigued her and she wanted to know more about them and why she had been so mistaken. What was it about them that they didn't conform to the stereotype? It was then that she realised that sitting behind her curtain was doing her no good and resolved that she must get out more and stop being so obsessed with the dog-owning public. After all, just because she wasn't a dog lover, she had to admit that people got a lot of pleasure out of their pets. So, she went into the scullery to bring out the pots in which she had planted her daffodil bulbs. They were sprouting well and she wanted to get them out front before the Easter mob arrived. She opened the door and there, on her step, was a big, steaming heap. As she turned to go and get the shovel, a voice called out to her from the lane.

"Hello. How are you? Not seen you for a while." It was the daughter of a woman she knew in the village.

"I'm fine, thanks. But look at this."

"Oh, dear," said the girl and grimaced at the mess. "I'm just going for a walk up to the falls."

"What you need," said Sarah, with a slight hint of sarcasm, "is a dog to take up there."

"Yes, I know. In fact, we are getting one next week," gushed the girl. "A chocolate labrador."

"I don't like chocolate," said Sarah, staring fixedly down at the dog shit.

The Farmer's Wife

ALICE needed to get out, to have fresh air blowing around her. As she left the farmhouse, the dog ran to join her but, today, she just wanted to be on her own. So she shouted to her son, Edwin, to call the collie back. She had been so distressed and distracted this past few weeks that she hadn't really noticed that spring had arrived at last after a hard winter. It was always a little later up on the moorland but, as she went down the hill, there were bright daffodils all along the grass verge nodding to her. This pleased her inordinately. It was almost as if they had been sent to cheer her up.

It was the kind of weather that she loved best. That time of year when winter had been banished, the earth was beginning to smell sweet again, green buds were showing in the hedgerow and the sky was a forget-me-not blue with cotton wool clouds moving slowly in the gentle breeze, casting brief shadows on the surrounding hills. Their early lambs, already fattening, were scampering and gambolling in that carefree manner that only the young possess.

Walking along, she thought of how she and Tom had built up the farm over the years. Indeed, the fields on both sides of the road were theirs, right down to the valley bottoms and they had had a good living from their sheep. She was proud and glad that their sons, Edwin, George and Alfie, were following in their footsteps as farmers so that the farm would be safe for another generation or even longer. So many young folk had left the land and it made her sad to think that age-old traditions of farming and husbandry were being lost, perhaps forever.

When she first came to this place as a young bride of eighteen, sixty years ago, she didn't like it. It seemed sparse and wild compared to the dairy farm with its lush green fields where she had grown up. There was so much sedge grass, which meant inhospitable, boggy land, but she had come to love it passionately for its wide vistas and the sense it gave you of being on top of the world, safe in one's own kingdom. With a great deal of hard work, they had improved the land and now she could not imagine a life elsewhere.

After their marriage, she had moved into Tom's family farm, with his parents, who were only too pleased to have younger hands to lighten the work, and when they passed away, the farm was left to Tom, as the eldest son. But she had never, for one moment, felt alone or isolated in their high moorland farm, for all the farmers around knew each other. In fact, they were often related and there was a great sense of community and always help in times of trouble. It occurred to her that most of her close friends were from farming families. Indeed, the nature of farming meant that there was not much time for socialising and fripperies for there was always a job to be done. So, trips to the hairdressers and for idle, indulgent shopping were very rare and it seemed to her that she and her friends were a race apart from some other women that she knew. They were practical, sensible, hard-working girls, with their feet firmly on the ground and a deep connection to the land. She smiled, for she still thought of them as girls because she had grown up with them and yet they were the same age as she was. How time flies, but where to? What's it all for?

As she turned a corner in the lane, the village came into view down below in the valley and she could see the square tower of the church. The sight of the church always made her feel grounded and secure. It was the place of so many family occasions; christenings, weddings, funerals, burials, harvest festivals, church fêtes and dances. The churchyard was full of headstones marking the resting places of members from both of their families and, judging by the flowers on the various graves whenever she visited there, local people still kept up a link with the past generations. She liked that; the fact that you didn't die when you died, as it were. She wasn't sure whether there was still the same respect for the dead in the towns and cities, which was a shame. She would have hated to live in a big town or a city. No room to breathe and think. No green fields. No air.

Suddenly, Alice became aware of a commotion in the trees as she passed by. It was the starlings. Bless them. They always appeared to be so sociable and friendly towards each other. They gladdened her heart. Then it seemed that all the birds around her had woken to spring and were calling out to each other, looking for a mate, making choices, settling down to build nests. This made her think of her own courtship days. She had met Tom at a barn dance at the church hall when she was sixteen. She knew who he was, but had never spoken to him as he was several years older than she was and mixed with a crowd of older lads. He was one of a family of five, three girls and two boys, and was good-looking, medium-height and not too stocky. Just right, she had thought. She watched him as he moved around the dance hall. Everyone greeted him, old and young alike, and he had a natural, easy way with people. She liked that.

Alice was sitting talking with her friends, drinking lemonade, when Tom came over and asked her to dance. She was flattered that he had singled her out. But this wasn't really surprising as Alice was very pretty. She was petite with red-gold curly hair and bright blue eyes. She had grown up in a family of four children in which she was the only girl and was the apple of her parents' eyes. However, she had not been spoiled and was really unaware of how she looked, which made her an attractive person to be with and to be friends with.

"You're Jack Beresford's daughter, aren't you?" Tom asked.

"Yes, I am," said Alice.

"He's the best drystone waller there is," Tom said. "You can tell his work anywhere. Wonderful skill that."

She was pleased that the conversation had started like this. It showed a respect for the older generation and for traditional skills. He was nice, really nice. She also noticed that he was a very good dancer. He had natural rhythm and balance, which made it so easy to talk while they moved around the floor. She didn't want the dance to end and apparently neither did he and so they danced together all evening. After that Tom and Alice were a couple. She loved the way he courted her. He was mannerly, in a slightly old-fashioned way, and extremely romantic and seemed in no hurry to take liberties with her, for which she was grateful. They were married in the local church, on a hot June day, just after her eighteenth birthday and she had never looked back. As she got to know his family, she found that they all had the same quiet dignity and reserve. They welcomed her into their bosom and she had always been grateful for their friendship and support.

The road was beginning to descend quite steeply now and, over to her left, her favourite landmark came into view. It was a limestone outcrop, known locally as the Dragon's Back because of the white spurs sticking out along its ridge. It was their faithful waymarker. When it appeared on the road home, they knew there was not far to go; a bit like a welcoming friend, or a favourite dog. It was also the place where Tom had proposed to her. One spring evening, he had taken Alice for a walk and as they went along he collected some primroses and other spring flowers from the hedgerow banks. At the top of the steep hill, he went down on one knee and asked her to marry him. So really it was their sacred hill. A place where they often went on anniversaries. Special. And it would be there long after they had all gone. She liked to think that the world carried on without you while you lay quietly somewhere, all the worries of the world cast off forever. It was part of that great cycle called life. No need to be sad.

Then, her thoughts turned to her sons. What would they do with their lives when their parents were gone? Edwin would have the farm. At present, he lived in a cottage nearby and worked on the farm with his dad. He was married to a very pleasant girl and had a family of his own, so that was all right. George was married to a 'bonnie lass', as Tom called her, whose father had asked him to go and live on their farm with a view to taking it on later, so he was settled. Now, Alfie, he was a different proposition. Alice wasn't sure that his heart was really in farming. He liked working with engines and farm machinery, but looking after the land always seemed like hard work to him and he did what he had to do grudgingly. So Alice wasn't sure about him. What is more, his wife, Pat, was difficult to get on with really. She wasn't a country girl and a good night out with the girls appeared to be her favourite pastime. They would have to work it out for themselves. The younger generation was different these days. She just hoped that she and Tom had given them the right principles, but nothing is certain. In fact, whatever happened in the distant future wouldn't be her concern.

All of a sudden, Alice came over faint, so she steadied herself against a gate post. Phew! What was that? Then she realised that she had had no breakfast, not even a drink, and had walked too far. Now, the hill that she had walked down so easily looked like an insurmountable mountain and she was overwhelmed with fatigue. She leant against the gatepost and bent over to clear her head. Just then, a camper van came up the hill with a young couple inside and they stopped to ask Alice if she was okay. She said that she had felt a bit dizzy but was all right now. They offered to give her a lift up the hill, which she accepted gratefully. Once she was seated inside and buckled up, they asked her where she lived and she pointed to the topmost farm, way up the hill. Then, she turned to the couple and said, "My husband died this morning. I will be all right, won't I?"

My Burma Boys

AS she waited in the long queue, Katie had time to look around. Lately, she had become fascinated by hair; women's hair, that is. In fact, she was making a study of it. Not in the academic sense, but more in a sociological kind of way for her own personal interest. For a start, she was amazed at the number of people who coloured their hair; young and old. No one seemed satisfied these days with the colour they were born with. Her 'field studies' were best undertaken in static crowds, like at bus stops, railway stations or audiences at concerts. Then, she would count how many women had altered their natural hair colour and, sometimes, it was as much as ninety per cent. This proportion was astonishing. She also noticed that all this messing about, as she called it, with their hair had made it thin and wispy. Nowadays, you hardly ever saw a full head of wavy, glossy hair glowing with health. But if you went to France, for example, flowing manes seemed to be everywhere. Was the thin hair down to all those bottles of colour or did the French have a better diet? It depressed her just thinking about it. And what's more, everyone seemed to be blonde these days. Grey hair was to be covered up as soon as it appeared. Well, at least that's what the adverts advised and self-interestedly promoted. Her own hair had been jet-black and was now silver and it had never seen a bottle.

Standing idly there getting rather impatient and musing about hair and blondes, she was suddenly reminded of a day, many years ago, sometime in the early 1970s, when she was standing in just such a queue as today and an older woman in front of her struck up a conversation. She was well made-up and had peroxide-blonde hair, which she wore in what used to be called 'bangs' in the 1940s. There was something slightly anachronistic about her look, which intrigued Katie, and she was forcibly reminded of Gracie Fields, with her blonde bangs and her turban, singing along with her chums in the factory in all those wartime films.

As an amateur student of human nature, Katie firmly believed that people's looks had a defined period in which they were at their best; a shelf-life, as it were. It was almost as if you had been given a time slot at birth; a brief spell when you would look your best and, when it expired, it was downhill all the way. She had known two girls at school who were perfect examples of this. One was an absolutely beautiful, angelic child with white-blonde curls, bright blue eyes and dimpled cheeks, a Shirley Temple in fact. But you knew, just by looking at her, that this look would have expired by the time she was eight. At the other end of the scale, there was Katie's friend, Janice, who, as a thirteen-year-old, was dumpy and podgy, but she was destined to come into her own as an attractive, stately matron around the age of fifty. Katie thought that, in the long run, this was probably the best slot to have been given. Then there was the other thing about lives. She had often met people who, because of either extreme happiness or sadness, had got stuck in a certain moment in their lives and had never moved on. For some reason, the woman in front had obviously stayed in the 1940s, the wartime years, and, as they chatted, Katie discovered the reason why.

"Oh, I wish they would get a move on," the woman exclaimed. "I'm making tea for my Burma boy and he will think I have forgotten him. I used to look after quite a few of them, bit of shopping, cleaning, dusting and polishing, and cooking, but there's only one left now."

"What do you mean, Burma boys?" asked Katie somewhat mystified, for she had never heard such an expression before.

"Well, you see," said the woman, "I was a nurse during the war, looking after wounded soldiers at Thorn Hall. I cared for the sick men who had been repatriated from Burma. Terrible to see it was. I know I shouldn't say it, given the suffering they went through, but that was the best time of my life, looking after my Burma boys."

And Katie could tell by the animated way the woman spoke about that period, when she would have been in her twenties, that she had wanted to stay there, in that most fulfilling time of her life, and had done so willingly.

Katie could see it all so vividly. She was able to image those wartime days and how that young, good-looking woman with spirit would have been a tonic for those sick men, who had been through hell. She had a great warmth and kindness about her that would have wrapped around them like a comfort blanket. Katie could also see that she would not have been shy and would have liked to flirt gently with those men who were fit enough to join in, and enjoy watching them be made human again by the contact. In fact, Rita, for that was her name, would have seen it as part of her role as a nurse to give them hope and make them feel not just human, but like men again, young, virile and strong, as they were when they left for war.

During Rita's time among her Burma boys, Katie guessed that there probably would have been one or two who became special to her. Perhaps there was one, more than anyone else, to whom she had given her heart. For, while they had been talking, Katie had noticed that Rita did not wear a wedding ring. She could see this man in her mind's eye. He was tall, slim and good-looking with fine features and fair hair, and he had a diffident, attractive manner about him. An officer perhaps who was drawn to this young, blonde with her infectious laugh and eternal optimism, but who was also extremely capable, intelligent and wise.

Rita would have pushed him around the grounds in his wheelchair when it was fine and his health had improved and a deep bond would have formed between them in the months that he spent at Thorn Hall. Yet, inevitably, the day would have come when he was fit enough to be returned whole to the bosom of his family; to his wife and children who could not wait to have him back. And so Rita had stayed in the 1940s, keeping alive a connection with her one true love through her care of her Burma boys.

Katie wanted to ask Rita many more questions about her fascinating life, get to know her better, become a friend even, but their conversation came to an end when there was, at last, movement in the queue as problems up ahead had been sorted out. As she reached the checkout, Rita turned to Katie, clasped her hand and said, "It's been lovely talking to you, dear. Take care of yourself and, remember, enjoy yourself as much as you can, but stop when you have had enough."

With that, she waved a cheery goodbye and went off to feed her Burma boy.

Suddenly, Katie was jolted out of her reverie because her own present-day queue was on the move at last. Was that really fifty years ago? She could hardly believe it. But, she had certainly heeded Rita's sound advice from that day long ago and it had served her well.

Brotherly Love

HE was the eldest in the family of six; two boys and four girls. He was intelligent and good looking with dark hair and big brown eyes. Growing up, Theresa was extremely proud of him as her older brother. Indeed, girls in her class were always angling for invitations to her house so that they could meet him. At mass on a Sunday, she noticed how some contrived to sit near him or happened 'accidentally' to bump into him on the way out of church. One girl even admitted that she had found out when he went to confession and was often there, just in case. But he never even noticed them and, more to the point, he never noticed Theresa either. In fact, he acted like an only child.

No matter what she did - walked on her hands, won prizes for swimming or running, or came top in spelling competitions - he appeared to be unaware of her existence. She used to pester him to let her and her friend go out with him and his pals because they always seemed to do exciting and dangerous things. Then, one day, surprisingly, he relented. He said that the gang was going to the 'haunted house' and that they could come but, "Don't tell Mum." To get to the ruined house, by the track across the fields, it was necessary to negotiate a way carefully through some old lime pits. So, two of the gang agreed to give Theresa and her friend piggy-backs. You had to be very careful there, they said, because, between the large tufts of solid grass, on which they were making their way, were pools of slimy, pale-green, whitish water which, Theresa was told, could burn off your flesh in a matter of minutes. Halfway across, the two boys stopped and dumped her and her friend on their own individual clumps of grass and leaped off laughing to join their chums. So they waited there, stranded and too scared to move, imagining a terrible fate if they slipped, all the while hoping some passer-by might happen along and rescue them. But they were there for about two hours until the boys came back for them. She knew that her brother was the instigator of this 'prank' to stop her pestering him and his friends once and for all, but she noticed how he had just stood there laughing, without getting involved in it. Her fear or terror at being left there in danger did not seem to affect him at all. So much for brotherly love.

A few years later, when Theresa was about twelve, out of the blue, her brother offered to take her to watch their local football club. She was so pleased that he had noticed her at last and was determined to act in an adult way and not cause him any bother. She felt privileged. However, there was a man in the crowd behind her who kept rubbing himself up against her. So she told her brother and his reply was, "Well, just move away from him." He said this almost as if he thought she was encouraging the man's attention. In that instant, she realised that she would never be able to turn to him for protection. Most brothers or fathers that she knew would have pushed the man away, threatened him or gone for an official, but not her brother. She had yet again been brought to understand that he had absolutely no interest whatsoever in her well-being.

As he grew older, her brother took up cycling. He joined a club and, with the other members, he would go out on practice runs on Saturdays and be involved in races and time-trials on Sundays. After practice, he would bring some of his mates back to their house for a cup of tea and their mother's scones, which were famous. This was great for Theresa and her sisters because, this way, they met some rather good-looking, fit young men, in tight cycling shorts. And, as it was always late Saturday afternoon when the lads were crowded in their kitchen, it was also the time when she would be getting ready to go out dancing and so her hair had been washed and curled and she would be looking her best. Some of the lads did notice her and one actually asked Theresa out on a date. She accepted, in spite of the fact that her brother had said that, on no account was she to go out with any of his cycling friends, presumably because he knew what they got up to when they were out on the town. She was a little surprised that he had even bothered to show any concern about this.

Theresa was seventeen and felt she was old enough to be taken to a jazz club in the city centre. She loved jazz but was worried that someone might notice she was under-age and she would not be admitted to the club. So, she borrowed a white, tight-fitting dress from her sister, painted her nails bright red and put on her highest heels. There was, in fact, no trouble from the doorman and Phil, her date for the night, was a perfect gentleman. She was loving the atmosphere - good music, dim lights, cigarette smoke and dancing - when, who should come down the steps but her brother. "Damn it. I'm in for it now," thought Theresa. But he didn't seem to mind her being there with one of his cycling mates.

He nodded to Phil, gave her a cursory glance, got himself a drink from the bar and then sat down to join them. He and Phil talked in a desultory fashion about bikes, racing and the music for about half-an-hour and then he suddenly exclaimed, pointing at her, "It's you." Theresa didn't know whether to laugh or cry. Either she looked so grown-up that he really didn't recognise her, which was great, or he still didn't really notice her at all. She had to admit to herself that it was probably the latter. He was the absolute limit and useless as a big brother.

When he was in his early twenties, he went off to university. Then, he emigrated with the 'brain drain' to America. In the meantime, Theresa got married and had a family, so she only met up with him when he came home on infrequent visits and there was a family gathering to celebrate his brief return to the fold. Away from home, in the States, he was able to reinvent himself and become an only child He had a good job, dabbled in property, had a yacht on San Francisco Bay, made and lost several fortunes and had many friends from different walks of life. You could say he had it all. There were many girl friends and some long-standing relationships, but he never seemed able to commit to any one woman in particular. He was too selfish or not interested enough in another person to care.

One time, Theresa and her husband were invited to a wedding in Los Angeles. As she had never been to America, they arranged a three-day detour to San Francisco to meet up with her brother; to see where he lived, get a flavour of the kind of life he led out there and do some sightseeing. When they arrived, they received a message to say that he had had an invitation to go 'up country' with some friends and would be back in a few days. This left them with just one day to catch up with him. Her husband was furious, but Theresa should have known. When he finally did turn up, they ended up paying for his dinner, instead of being treated as his guests. She decided that it was time to give up trying to get him to notice her, to treat her as an adult with a life which he might find interesting, if only he bothered to ask her any questions.

And so the years crept by with hardly any communication between them. Then one day, when he was in his late sixties, Theresa received a phone call from a friend to say that her brother had been found in his apartment after suffering a massive stroke. He was in intensive care. She went over immediately with one of her sisters, but sadly he died just four days later. They had three weeks in which to find friends who would help them with all the foreign bureaucracy, settle his financial affairs and organise a funeral. Going through his belongings, their brother's life was laid bare. It was indeed a post-mortem. There were inches of dust in the apartment and his clothes were threadbare but the cupboard was full of vitamin pills. There was a strange anomaly between the general lack of care about some things and his obvious desire to keep fit and healthy. It saddened Theresa. His colleagues in the real estate agents where he worked, did not even know that he had sisters and a brother. He had never talked about them. Surprisingly, he was still a practising Catholic and an active member of his local church and was, indeed, very well thought of there. In fact, he was their star fundraiser. This conflicted with the edgy life he seemed to have led, which was revealed in his diary. There was obviously another darker side to his life, into which

Theresa and her sister decided not to delve too deeply. If that was how he had chosen to live his life, who were they to judge? A neighbour told them that he liked their brother because "he did stuff". They didn't really want to know. Not now. It was too late.

The funeral was attended by many people and Theresa and her sister, being the only family members present, had to find some words to say about this brother whom they hardly knew and who had never really known them. Theresa read a poem by Antonio Machado about God asking someone what they had done with their garden during their life and her sister talked of brotherhood and his relationship with his family and his church. It was sad for many reasons but, for Theresa, in some ways it seemed a little hypocritical. He was virtually a stranger. What did she know about him? What right did she have to speak about him?

After the service, the church members provided a buffet and, later, the sisters invited some of their brother's friends back to the apartment for a drink. As Theresa was searching in a drawer for a corkscrew, she found a letter from their mother written to her brother some time before she died. It was in that distinctive handwriting of hers and told him about the funeral of one of their favourite uncles and it could have been describing the one that had just taken place. The details of the day were so similar. It was uncanny and also extremely poignant.

And so Theresa and her sister left him there; the brother with whom she had never really had a conversation, never shared thoughts or dreams. His ashes were 'inurnated', as the American funeral director called it, some days after they had flown back home. They had to leave before this could be organised because their flight was already booked. The urn was placed in a small niche in a wall in a cemetery, high on a hill, looking out over a country in which her brother had lived for most of his adult life and where he had not one single, living relative. Apparently, none of his friends were available to attend the ceremony.

The Brick Wall

TO say that her mother-in-law was a difficult woman was to put it mildly. Six months after they met, Liz and Rob decided to get married. They were to move to London, where Rob had already started a new job, and begin their life together. So, in order to establish her credentials as a good daughter-in-law, Liz went to visit his mother several times in the weeks leading up to the wedding. It meant quite a long detour for her after work in the city centre. She had to take a bus out to the suburbs and then a bus back into the city before taking the train home, which was about sixteen miles away. But it was worth it if she could make friends with Rob's mum at the outset of her married life.

However, on one evening visit, she was just coming back from the kitchen, when she heard her future mother-in-law, Martha, saying to a neighbour, who had popped in for a chat, "I don't know who she thinks she is coming here and looking down on me." Liz was dumbfounded. She had never done any such thing. She didn't even think like that. It was so unjust. As she entered the room, Martha smiled at her, as if nothing had been said, and introduced her to the friend, while handing Liz a cup of tea and a slice of cake. Then Martha showed the neighbour all the things she had kindly collected together to give to the young couple. Liz decided to act as if she had not heard what Martha had said and gushed with thanks about her generosity.

The following Friday, just a week before their December wedding, Liz received a phone call from Martha at work. The police had towed Rob's car away for being parked too long on the street, but she wasn't to tell him. It would be a surprise for him when he got back on the day before the 'big day'. But, of course, Liz would have to tell him. They needed the car to go into the city to get married. After the wedding, it would have to be packed with all their belongings, ready for the long drive south. He would simply have to come home a day early in order to go and retrieve the car from the police pound.

When Liz arrived at Martha's for her weekly visit the following Wednesday, she was met by a furious tirade.

"How could you betray me like this? It is treacherous of you. I told you not to tell him. I certainly won't be coming to the wedding now and, in any case, I have nothing new to wear."

"What a mess, what a woman," thought Liz and she could see that, in the future, she would have to put up with much more of this.

They only had a simple wedding with a few guests and her parents made a wedding breakfast for them after the ceremony. After they had waved goodbye to her parents, they went back to Martha's to collect their belongings and say farewell. Rob entered the house and, as he walked down the hall, she heard her new mother-in-law shout, "Don't bring her in here. I hate her." Liz was too shocked for words and so began her married life.

That winter was one of the coldest on record and Liz and Rob were unable to travel north to visit parents until Whitsuntide when the weather warmed up. They stayed with his mother because there was no room for them at her parents' house. Martha did not speak one word to Liz. All her conversation was directed at Rob. In the mornings, she would burst into their bedroom, without knocking or speaking, and plonk a tray full of food down on the bed. There was enough food to overface even a famished bricklayer. Sometimes Liz could not manage to eat it all and when they brought the tray down later, Martha would burst into tears when she saw that her offering had apparently been rejected. This scenario would be re-enacted every time they went to stay, at Christmas, at Easter, at Whitsun, and in the summer, and Liz never said a word about Martha's behaviour to Rob and Rob never challenged his mother about her treatment of his new wife.

At Easter, just over a year after their marriage, they travelled north to visit Martha. Easter was very early that year and it was very cold. On Easter Monday morning, when they were due to go back home, Rob found that the fuel pipe on his car had fractured in the hard frost and all the petrol had leaked away. He called the breakdown service and, as they needed the car quickly, he went with the repair man so he could bring the car back the minute it was done. Liz was left with Martha; Martha who had suddenly somehow become mute. It was a bank holiday and all the shops were shut. The pavements were lethal with ice and so there was nowhere for Liz to go. The house, being an old Victorian house, had no central heating and most of the rooms were glacially cold. The lounge was marginally warmer because the fire had been lit in there the day before and there was still some residual heat in the room. So, if she didn't actually want to freeze to death, Liz had no option but to put on an extra jumper and sit by the fireplace opposite this silent, obdurate woman. She noticed that the grate had been cleaned out and the fire reset for later, but Martha had no intention of lighting it for Liz's benefit.

Because it was a holiday weekend, there were no sounds coming in from the street. No vans, lorries or cars, and the cold was keeping the children indoors. Liz had not brought a book with her and there were no newspapers or magazines around so she could not distract herself by burying her head in their pages. As this was not her own house, she was too polite and cowed by this woman to switch on the television or the radio and she knew that Martha was certainly not going to do that for her entertainment. As they sat there in silence, Martha sat knitting a shawl for her neighbour's expected new grandchild and Liz marvelled at her dexterity and the fact that pure lace was appearing under her fingers and she was not even using a pattern. She must have been taught that skill as a country child. It was wonderful. Surely someone who could make something so beautiful must have a heart somewhere, even a soul, so why was she behaving so cruelly towards her daughter-in-law? The only thing she could think of was that Martha was jealous. Liz had stolen her only son. And not being old or wise enough yet, Liz could not understand the pain of that loss and so could not sympathise with her.

Normally, Liz was a spirited young woman who was not afraid to speak her mind if things were not right, but, at twenty-one, she had not yet learnt strategies for dealing with Martha's kind of behaviour. It was completely foreign to her. She had come from a loving home where kindness and ease were the norm. There were often parties and much laughter.

Her uncles and aunts were good fun and she and her siblings played with their cousins in harmony and friendship. For once in her life, Liz had nothing to say. Even if she had, she didn't think the words would come out in this arctic atmosphere; they would be frozen in the air as soon as they left her mouth. And so they sat there, where the only sound breaking the silence was a ticking clock. It reminded Liz of one time long ago when her mother had taken her to visit a friend with some important news; about a death, she thought it was. She was shut away in the front parlour for ages with only the ticking of a grandfather clock to keep her company, while the grown-ups talked away in the back kitchen. She was reminded now of the strange silence of that day. It had the same kind of funereal air.

Every now and again, Martha would get up and go into the kitchen to make a cup of tea. She would come back in and slap a mug down on the table in front of Liz without a word. As the hours went by, no food was offered, no comfort given, and all the time, the brick wall between them got higher and higher and more impenetrable. It was almost as if there were actually a physical wall between the two women. It was like a prison wall and Liz felt as if she had been bound and gagged. She was stunned by the way that one person's behaviour could create such a solid barrier and how she could be so affected by it that it had altered her own behaviour. It was frightening really. She had been rendered powerless by silence. And so it went on for three long hours until Rob returned with the car and the spell of the Wicked Witch of the North was broken. When she stood up to leave, Liz grabbed the matches from the mantelpiece and set the fire aflame, feeling an immense sense of liberation.

Guilty as Charged

I WENT to court today to contest a parking fine which I thought was unwarranted, as I had had every right to park when and where I did, and I wanted an opportunity to speak in my defence. What theatre! What human inadequacy! When I arrived, I was shown into a waiting room by an over-officious, middle-class woman, who looked as if she made instant judgements on everyone she ushered in. Inside the room, there was an older couple and, sitting staring at the ground away down the end of the waiting area, a young lad with ripped jeans and a wispy beard, who looked as if he needed a good meal. As I waited there, in silence, I speculated on what offences these disparate people might have committed.

The couple fascinated me. They were perhaps in their late sixties and sat there unspeaking, as they probably had done most of their married life. They were soberly dressed. He wore a threadbare tweed suit and carried a flat cap. She was dressed in a drab, brown-beige outfit and wore a dark-brown pillbox hat, which was clamped firmly down on her permed hair. She had placed her shopping bag between herself and her husband like a barrier and, in the hour that I sat there, not a word passed between them. They looked like people who might have owned a small shop of some kind in the town and had spent their life counting the pennies and never giving anything away if they could help it. There was a loveless air about them. Probably never had children.

Suddenly, the door was flung open and a big shambling, bull-like man burst into the room, escorted by a police officer, who was trying to restrain him. He seemed to have a constant nervous tremor and looked around with wild, staring eyes. On seeing the woman, he made straight for her and threatened to "smash her face in whether or not she was his sister". The policeman had to pull him off her. I looked at the woman. She did not move, showed no emotion whatsoever, and stared fixedly at the wall on the other side of the room. Nor did this outburst provoke any comment between the couple. The wild man was swaying violently and flailing his arms around, muttering darkly that she was selfish and had cheated him out of their father's inheritance. He attempted once more to strike her. He shouted that she owed him £8000, which he would "have out of her". But there was absolutely no response from the couple. Nothing. She did not raise an eyebrow, shrug a shoulder or make some gesture in the way of an apology or excuse to the others in the room for the disruption and embarrassment of it all. What incredible control, or perhaps she had never felt anything except the will to survive. It made me wonder about their childhood, these strange incompatible people.

As the time ticked by without any one of us being called into court, I stood up and looked at the charge sheet for the day, which was displayed on the notice board. It appeared that the young man was up before the magistrate for sixteen offences, all for breaking and entering on several occasions at properties on the same street. What kind of brain works away in such a mind? What desperation, what hopelessness motivates him? What future could there possibly be for him? The futility of it all made me despair.

I was found guilty. Madam 'know-all' usher in her black court gown informed me that I had got off lightly.

Vanishing Trick

FIONA had known Vanessa all her life, or so it seemed. They met, aged five, on the first day of school when they were seated next to each other. From that day on, they were inseparable. Fiona adored her friend. She was so beautiful. She was taller than Fiona and had short, dark-brown hair, with a fringe which framed her oval face, and gorgeous grey-blue eyes. In fact, she had a slightly oriental look which made her an even more exotic creature to Fiona. Above all, Vanessa was great fun, always on the look out for comic situations or making funny remarks about things. She was a natural actress. Also, there were benefits from being Vanessa's best friend. Not only was she the most beautiful girl in the class, in the school for that matter, but she had a slightly imperious manner about her, because she was tall for her age, and she could always think of a quick answer when someone was being horrid to her. So, as long as Fiona stayed within her orbit, she was safe from the nastiness of some of the other children. Fiona loved school.

Somehow, Vanessa was always chosen to play the most important roles in school productions, be they entertainments put on for parents' evenings, end-of-term school plays, or Christmas pantomimes. And, naturally, she was nearly always the Virgin Mary in the nativity plays, with Fiona hovering around as one of the angels in the background. Fiona didn't mind playing second fiddle to her friend. She felt Vanessa deserved the attention because she was so lovely. But as they went up through the school, some teachers did mind for Fiona.

Fiona was pretty, but could never be called beautiful like Vanessa. But, she had a kind nature and was extremely bright. Several of the staff told her parents that they were worried that she was too attached to Vanessa, too much in her shadow and this was affecting her so that she wasn't achieving her potential. Therefore, they took pains to put the two girls in different groups, from time to time, so that Fiona could shine in her own right, and gain some sense of her own identity and recognise her talents. She, herself, was blissfully unaware of how much she was under the spell of her friend, Queen Vanessa. For that's how Fiona saw her friend, noble and regal. In fact, the class had been learning about the Egyptians and she saw Vanessa as the very reincarnation of the Queen of Sheba.

However, when the girls were eleven, they were separated for the first time in their lives. They both passed the eleven-plus exam but, for various reasons, they ended up going to different schools. Fiona missed Vanessa very much, but they would meet up in the town on a Saturday and exchange news about their schools and their new friends. Their talk was often about how much they loved sport, tennis especially, and so Vanessa persuaded Fiona to ask her parents if she could join their local tennis club. That way, they could see more of each other. As Vanessa was already a member, she had gained a toe-hold in her new realm and so, when Fiona joined, she was once again cast in the role of handmaiden. But she didn't mind. She liked to watch Vanessa putting on her show and enjoyed seeing how people admired her and, indeed, was pleased to have the privileged role as her friend.

Vanessa had a gorgeous figure and lovely long legs which were shown off to perfection by skimpy tennis wear, and she knew it. In her time as a member of the junior team, she had gathered a retinue of suitors around her, all willing to do her bidding. Fiona was now detached enough to be able to see it as a performance but she wasn't jealous of all the attention Vanessa was getting. As far as Fiona was concerned, things were as they had always been. Besides, since leaving junior school, Fiona had gained a sense of her own identity and was a good tennis player. In fact, she was often paired with Vanessa in doubles matches, when she had an opportunity to show off her skills and catch the eye of several admirers for herself.

Among these admirers was a lad called Max. He was tall and rangy with a tangled mop of brown-blond curly hair and a quirky sense of humour, which he shared with Fiona. Latterly, he had been one of Vanessa's followers but, gradually, he had begun to notice Fiona and the neat way she moved on the court and her determination to win. She was also good fun and did not crave constant attention like her friend. For a while, Fiona was oblivious to a change in Vanessa's attitude towards her. She became more off-hand with her, making excuses that she had to go and talk to someone, that she hadn't time for a coffee after a match and suggesting less frequently that they meet in town for a chat. Suddenly, it dawned on Fiona that her friend was jealous. This was a new experience for her. She realised that she had broken the unspoken rule and stopped playing fealty to the Queen. Their relationship had undergone a sea change.

Over the next few years, as they went up through high school, Fiona still saw Vanessa at the club and met up from time to time for a coffee. Then, after final exams, there came the question of choosing careers and serious boyfriends also appeared on the scene. Fiona decided that she wanted to teach French and Spanish and so enrolled on a course. Vanessa, not being so academically minded, chose to go into the business world. She landed a job in an upmarket art gallery, where they sold not only pictures but the most beautiful pottery, glassware and sculptures. It was an environment that suited her perfectly and was where she met elegant and sophisticated people who had the money to spend on the expensive *objets d'art* the gallery sold. Naturally, it was not long before one of these said rich people noticed Vanessa and whisked her off to his castle, as his bride and queen.

Meanwhile, Fiona qualified as a teacher. She had met Rob at university and they were now married and had two children. As her life was so vastly different from the one Vanessa was leading, they very rarely saw one another. She heard snippets about her from various friends, such as how many children she had, where they were living, what an expensive lifestyle she led. "Good for her," Fiona often thought without a trace of envy. "Horses for courses." Then, she began to hear that there was trouble in paradise and that a divorce was on the cards. She wondered what could possibly have gone wrong but, as they were not in touch, she didn't like to intrude. However, she did feel sorry that things had not turned out well for Vanessa, who always seemed to have everything.

When Fiona's children were old enough not to need her constant attention, she joined a local women's discussion group for some mental stimulation and a chance to make some new friends. One evening, just before a talk on the novels of Jane Austen, who should walk into the room but Vanessa, dressed like a million dollars. And, as of old, there was the usual flutter of acolytes around the high priestess, with people offering her the best seat near the speaker, handing her cups of tea and pieces of cake, welcoming her into their fold. So, it was some while before she noticed Fiona. She swept across the room regally and made a great fuss of her old friend. "Well, what a lovely surprise. Fancy seeing you here. You must tell me everything." Her delivery was slow and well-modulated and Fiona noted a touch of accent modification in it all. As usual, she was playing to the gallery and people were impressed that Fiona knew such an obviously high-status woman; so perfectly coiffed and stylish.

Fiona was a little irritated that Vanessa had appeared on her patch and sincerely hoped that she did not think that her old friend could still be impressed by 'the performance'. However, Fiona had to admit that she looked good; her hair was beautifully cut and still framed that lovely, oval face; the nails were manicured to perfection; the teeth had been professionally straightened and her clothes were expensive and wonderfully co-ordinated. In fact, it was all a fantastically contrived work of art. Eventually, when the talk had finished, they had time to sit and chat about what they had been doing in the intervening years. She learned that Vanessa was now divorced and had moved, with her three children, to a suburb not far away. Her husband had gone off with some rich widow who had inherited a substantial estate. Vanessa had received a generous settlement and so she was now adjusting to life as a single parent. However, she was still playing tennis and was, in fact, to be made lady president next season. Also, Fiona learned that one of Vanessa's sons was a fantastic player, winning cups at national and international junior championships. She was so proud of him. In fact, in the end, the conversation seemed to be about nothing but this child prodigy, Adam. Fiona wondered how Vanessa's other two children felt about the time, energy and money being spent on their sibling. But, then, that was Vanessa all over, still craving the limelight one way or another.

After they reconnected, Fiona and Vanessa met up from time to time and Fiona was sometimes persuaded to attend or help out at fundraising events at the tennis club that Vanessa and her committee organised. But, when Vanessa invited her to join her committee properly, Fiona used the excuse that she was bogged down with school work. "No way," thought Fiona, "I am not going back to being her willing slave again, taking orders from Lady Bountiful." However, in spite of being able to see the flaws in Vanessa's character, Fiona still liked her. She admired the way she had picked herself up after the divorce and had set about reinventing herself. She certainly had self-confidence and a positive attitude and she still made Fiona laugh.

One evening Fiona and her husband, Rob, were attending a tennis club charity ball organised by Vanessa, which was being held in a local Michelin-starred hotel. There were lots of people that Fiona knew from her teenage days, who had obviously made it in life. Husbands sported expensive suits and their wives were bedecked with jewels and dressed in the latest fashions. It was all very glittery and a little out of Fiona and Rob's usual comfort zone. Not because they didn't feel they could compete but because they were surrounded by the sort of people they would not usually choose to have as friends. "So this is Vanessa's real world," thought Fiona.

The evening was structured so that a meal was served first, then there was to be dancing and, at a set time, there was to be a raffle with wonderful prizes, donated by some of the richer members of the club. Fiona and her husband had opted to share their table with people that they did not know. When an older couple approached them and asked if they were in the right spot, Fiona said, "Yes, you certainly are. Please do join us." The couple were both wearing velvet capes over their formal evening dress and were obviously used to attending such prestigious events. When they were settled, Fiona introduced herself and Rob and they, in turn, replied that they were Jane and Andrew.

"How do you know Vanessa?" Jane asked Fiona.

"Oh, we go back a long way, " said Fiona. "We were five when we met on the first day at school."

"Wow," said Jane. "That's a lifetime. We got to know Vanessa and Peter when they bought the big house down the lane from us. We have been very close friends ever since; holidays together, sailing, travelling abroad. In fact, we often stayed at their house in Provence. Pity that they have divorced, but Vanessa often pops in. So, thankfully, we have not lost touch."

"Where do you live?" asked Fiona, just to make conversation, and Jane replied, "We live in a grace-and-favour house in the grounds of Huxton Manor. So we haven't had far to come. And where do you two live?"

Fiona replied, "Ashfield."

"Oh, do tell me," said Jane. "Do you have any niggs in Ashfield?"

Fiona was utterly dumbstruck that anyone could say such a thing, especially to two complete strangers, but, even more so, that they should even think such a thing. So this was a close friend of Vanessa's, a friend she obviously did not know at all? She looked at Rob and they silently agreed that conversation was no longer possible with such blatant racists. They made small talk with some people on the next table and feigned interest in what was going on around them and completely ignored the couple for the rest of the evening.

After this incident, Fiona watched her 'friend', who was sitting at what passed for the high table. It was stuffed with tennis club dignitaries, all laughing and patting each other on the back and she observed Vanessa minutely. She was smiling and dispensing largesse around her like confetti. The men were paying court and the women were fawning and obviously somewhat in awe of her. And, as Fiona observed the spectacle, with Jane's words still echoing in her ears, she was reminded of a scene in the film *Oh, What a Lovely War*, where a troupe of young, pretty dancing girls come on stage and sing 'We Don't Want to Lose You', enticing the young men in the audience to do their bit and join up for King and country. Immediately after this number, an older trooper comes on stage and sings 'I'll Make a Man of You', using sexual innuendo to stiffen their resolve, as it were. But as she is singing, she slowly turns into a repulsive, painted, hag-ridden old woman. The scales had been peeled from Fiona's eyes.

Consequently, whenever Vanessa contacted her after that evening, Fiona invented excuses not to meet up, or said she had to telephone the parent of a pupil in a few minutes if Vanessa had rung for a long chat. As far as she was concerned, the friendship was over. She felt sorry about it naturally but, somewhere on the journey of life, their paths had diverged and they had ended up in totally different universes. However, she still heard news of Vanessa from various friends and acquaintances and according to the gossip, some time previously, she had met and married a successful architect. He was English and had practices in both England and South Africa. He would spend six months in England and six months at his other practice. So when they married, they bought a *pied-à-terre* in England, not far from where Vanessa used to live after her divorce. This meant that she could see her children when she came back home. Richard, the new husband, had designed a superb, modern house for them on the coast near Cape Town. However, recently, Fiona had been intrigued by some talk that Vanessa had fallen out with her son, Adam. Apparently, friends told her, the rift was so deep that it could not be mended. Fiona was astonished. What could he possibly have done that Vanessa could not forgive? Try as she might, she could not find out.

Then one day, Fiona was at the local hospital for a routine check-up on her eyes, when to her surprise she saw Vanessa being wheeled along the corridor by a nurse. She was incredibly thin and had a patch over one eye. Fiona went up to her and touched her arm and said, "Oh, Vanessa, are you all right?" She realised immediately that it was a stupid thing to say. She obviously was not all right. In fact, it looked very bad indeed. Vanessa looked up and said, pitifully, "Not really". Fiona was stunned to see her beautiful friend so broken. When she got home, she rang around her friends and it turned out that Vanessa had an aggressive form of cancer and had not long to live. Four weeks later there was news of her death. It was unbelievably sad.

At the funeral, there were many friends from every part of Vanessa's life and the church was packed. People were chatting in hushed tones when, just before the service started, there was a sort of intake of breath from the congregation and people turned to see Adam, Vanessa's son, walking down the aisle with the most stunning black woman Fiona had ever seen. She was tall, regal and stylishly dressed and was holding hands with an equally beautiful, mixed-race child. "His wife," said the friend next to her. Now Fiona understood the falling out.

After the service, everyone was invited to attend a buffet lunch at the hotel next door. Fiona and Rob commiserated with the family and then circulated and greeted the people they knew, eventually sitting down for something to eat. Fiona got into conversation with the woman sitting next to her. She was Vanessa's type; immaculately dressed, hair beautifully cut and a restrained amount of expensive jewellery.

"Were you a friend of Vanessa's?" Fiona asked the woman.

"Yes," she replied. "We played golf together, what about you?"

"Oh, I knew her from our first day at school."

"So you must have known her really well," said the woman. "Did you ever go to their house in South Africa?" asked the woman.

"No," answered Fiona. "Our lives have been on different paths these past few years."

"Oh, you definitely should have," said Vanessa's friend. "It is out of this world. It's built right on the ocean, with stunning views out to sea and you never, ever see a black face. You would absolutely love it."

Sin of Omission

THEY both worked on the high street. He was a salesman for a wine merchants at the top end near the marketplace and she worked in a family-run travel firm lower down the street on the opposite side. They did not know each other but they had, as it were, 'clocked' each other. She would see him sometimes when she went to a café in the market place for a sandwich and he would be in there buying a snack to take out. She liked the way he dressed; well-cut suits, good shoes and a nice watch. He obviously took care of his body and probably, like her, went to the gym. There was a look of purpose about him, as if he knew what he wanted. But he didn't seem arrogant, just self-confident. Apart from all that, he was really good-looking. When he had first noticed her, he thought to himself, "Well, she's a bit of all right". She had a trim, neat little body, short, dark hair, which suited her, and lovely, slim legs. She, too, had a look about her of someone who knew what they were aiming for. For him, that was attractive and he wondered who she was. Then, quite fortuitously, he had the opportunity to find out.

By chance, one December, their respective firms had booked their Christmas parties on the same night at the same venue in the market square and they were seated on adjoining tables. Part way through the evening, Tony seized his opportunity and asked Maureen if she would care to dance. They hit it off instantly. In fact, they felt that they knew each other already, having had such a long time to study one another in passing. She had been right about him. He did go to the gym and it showed. He was well-toned and agile on his feet. He, in turn, appreciated her firm figure and liked the way she laughed at his jokes. After that night, they met frequently, going to dances, clubs and music festivals, and walking in the country. They got engaged a year later and married not long after.

They agreed, from the outset, that they did not want a family. Maureen and Tony came from similar backgrounds. Her father was a bricklayer who worked for a local building firm. However, he had developed a liking for the drink and was more often off work than at work. When he was drunk, he would get violent with her mother and, when Maureen was younger, she would try to keep her little sisters safe when things flared up. Eventually, she left home to share a flat with a girl she worked with and was determined to make a better life for herself. She had found the job with the travel agent when she was eighteen and absolutely loved it because it opened up new worlds for her. She was extremely good at what she did and promised herself often that one day she would be the one going on those expensive holidays that her clients booked.

Tony's father was a joiner, a skilled craftsman who was much in demand locally, but something had soured him in his younger days and made him churlish and difficult. He never had a single word of praise for Tony or his brother, no matter how hard they tried to please him or succeeded at school. So, quite early on, Tony was determined to make a success of his life and prove to his father that he had worth.

At eighteen, he was taken on by the wine merchants as a general dogsbody, with a view to being trained as a salesman. He was a quick learner and soon discovered that he could tell a excellent wine from a mediocre one. Gradually, he was given more responsibilities and soon became their top salesman. He loved his job and was well suited for it. His manner was affable and courteous and he was always smartly turned out, so the customers took to him straight away. But he was also extremely meticulous in keeping his paperwork up-to-date, delivering orders on time and knowing what the different clients might like or would be willing to try. His boss was proud of him.

By the time they had been married about fifteen years, they had built a nice, comfortable life for themselves. Tony been promoted to chief buyer, had shares in the firm and was due to take over the running of the business when his boss retired. Maureen now worked only three mornings a week at the travel agents and her remit was to arrange expensive and complicated travel tours for their very best clients. And, as she had always dreamed, they could now afford to take such holidays themselves. Tony was a member of the local golf club and the Rotary club and was on the board of the local football club. They both went to the gym regularly to keep themselves in trim. Maureen loved cooking and had attended many cookery classes so that she could play hostess when they gave dinner parties. She liked nothing better than to have an opportunity to show off their lovely home, which she polished and made sparkle to perfection when they had guests.

Their house, which they had bought about five years ago, was a large older one in a leafy part of town, standing in nearly an acre of garden. Over time, they had modernised every inch of it. The kitchen was stylish and minimalist with everything of the highest quality. It was black, white and chrome, and gadgetry heaven. Two years ago, they had added an annexe leading off the kitchen, which contained a guest bedroom with an en-suite shower room, a gym and a modest, indoor swimming pool, which opened out onto a terrace. There were also two quality cars in the garage. The whole thing gave them both satisfaction when they settled down in the evening after work to watch television or a film. They had made it and were quietly pleased with themselves.

Because of their early lives, neither of them had been brought up on a diet of romance or sentiment. They didn't go in for what they called 'sloppiness', but they loved each other deeply in their own way and had each other's back, as the saying goes. They knew what it had taken them to get so far. People found them to be good fun and very sociable, but deep down they were extremely private people and quite content with their own company. You could not call them hard or unfeeling. They gave freely of their time and money to people who genuinely needed their help and to charities they felt were worthwhile. They were just a practical and straightforward couple without airs and graces.

Over the years, Tony had built up a solid client base both at home and in Europe, so he made regular trips to France, Italy, Germany, Spain and Portugal, often staying away for four or five nights. Maureen enjoyed those times on her own because it allowed her to meet up with friends, eat her meals when she wanted and go to bed late if there was a film she wanted to watch. She lived a different rhythm for a few days and liked it. She presumed that Tony enjoyed his little trips too, his escapes from their normal routine, but she was always glad to see him safely back home.

However, sometimes, when Maureen was doing the laundry after Tony's trips abroad, she would find a faint smudge of lipstick on a shirt collar or get a whiff of an unfamiliar perfume. She wasn't jealous exactly, rather intrigued. Tony was not a demonstrative man. He kept his feelings under control. For example, he found it hard to tell her he loved her, but she knew that he did and she didn't need to be told. Their lovemaking had always been great, but it was more like a good workout than a romantic coupling and that suited them both. In this way, both of them kept their identities intact and their thoughts to themselves. The idea that Tony found satisfaction somewhere else made her think that perhaps she should give it a try. If he could play away, she might play away at home. Everything would be all right as long as she didn't do anything foolish and wreck what they had. And so she worked out a plan.

She decided that, whatever she got up to, it would be here at home. She did not fancy sordid meetings in hotels or, even worse still, assignations in cars when there was the possibility of being seen by people she knew. That was far too dangerous. No, the best way to have a little enjoyment would be with the tradesmen who came to the house. In a place like theirs, there was always something that needing seeing to, so no one would think it odd when a van drew up at the gate. She would always use tradesman from out of her area, so that they did not know her or Tony and she would probably only use them once, so there was no danger of someone getting serious about her. She didn't see the idea of having sex with workmen as lowering herself, for she came from the same working-class background as did most of the joiners, painters, gardeners and plumbers she might use. Finally, there were two golden rules. Firstly, they had to be married and, secondly, they must not object to using condoms. That way, if they had a wife and family they would be less likely to cause her trouble. They, like her she hoped, would be out for a bit of fun on a working day.

So far things had worked out well and she had had some memorable encounters. The arrangement of the annexe leading off the kitchen suited her perfectly. There was the guest bedroom just next door, with the shower room leading off it and then there was the swimming pool. Sometimes, if a bloke had been doing a hard, dirty job, like laying flagstones or digging out tree roots, she would suggest that he might like a swim to cool off. Then she would join him in the pool and enjoy whatever happened next. She found those times after a swim were the most exciting and surprising. And, actually, she had met some really nice men. More importantly, she always made a point of phoning Tony before she got involved in anything just to make sure he was on foreign soil and would not suddenly walk in and surprise her in the act. She knew as soon as she heard the ring tone whether he was abroad or not. Then, she would have a little chat about the job that needed doing and ask him if there was anything more that she needed to point out to the tradesman.

One day, a few weeks before she was due to give a large dinner party, she noticed that the ovens of the range cooker really needed a good clean and she didn't fancy kneeling down on the hard floor herself to scrub off all the grime. She must get someone in, and she would get it done when Tony was away on one of his trips so that he wouldn't be inconvenienced. So she casually asked around her friends if they knew of anyone. A colleague said that she had a friend who had used this man, who was an absolute miracle worker. The problem was that he lived quite a way off and she didn't know whether he came as far out as their area. It sounded perfect to Maureen. So she rang him and he agreed to do the job and gave her a quote.

Maureen knew from the outset if a bloke would be up for fun as soon as she opened the door. She would, first of all, look for the wedding ring and then give him a quick once-over before deciding whether it was worth a chance or whether even to bother. When Dave rang the bell, she knew at once that things would probably be all right. He was tall and not bad-looking, with a lopsided grin that spoke of someone who had been around and who might be open to suggestions. She took him into the kitchen and showed him what needed doing, made him a cup of tea, asked him how long the job might take and then left him to do what was necessary. There was some tidying up needed in the bedroom, papers to sort out in the study and the bathroom had to be cleaned. She worked out how long this might take her and the plan was to change into her swimwear around the time Dave would be almost finished. Then she would appear in the kitchen, as if on the way for a swim.

As she walked in, she let the bathing robe that she was wearing over her bikini drift provocatively open, and said casually, "I usually have a swim about this time so I thought I'd get ready before I came back down." As she brushed past him, ostensibly to look at his handiwork, he gave her a cheeky grin and, with the back of his index finger, gently caressed the S-curve of her waist and hip.

"Mmm, tasty," he said, raising an eyebrow.

"Game on," thought Maureen.

"Well, now let me see what miracles those magic fingers of yours have worked on my ovens," she said, as she bent down to inspect his handiwork, stringing out the tension a little longer. The ovens were gleaming and sparkling like never before and she was so pleased. But, as she stood upright, she noticed that the top of the cooker had not been cleaned.

"You've not done the burners," she said, somewhat dismayed.

"Oh, I don't do 'obs," said Dave.

"Well," thought Maureen, pulling the bathing robe tightly round her, "Game off. I am certainly not having sex with a bloke who drops his 'aitches."

"Now, what do I owe you," said Maureen, in her best business-like, no nonsense voice.

Instinct

NANCY had always had an instinct about people. From a very early age, she could tell the people she could trust; they didn't even need to speak. And, by the same token, she knew when someone was not honest or up to no good. Indeed, when she was a very young child in the pram, a passer-by said to her mother, "My, hasn't your child got an old stare." And this instinct had always served her well and kept her out of danger.

As a child, she had been left to roam freely around the countryside near her home with her brothers and sisters and friends. It was a safe environment. Most of the people she met were locals and hardly anyone had a car, so not many strangers came into her area. Danger came mainly from being too adventurous, like crossing the fast-flowing river on the green, slimy waterfall, tippling on high bars, daring each other to walk into railway tunnels or swinging over ravines on ropes tied to trees. You judged how much fear you wanted to experience and so everything was under your control. However, one day a different kind of danger entered Nancy's life.

She attended school in the nearby town and, when she was about nine years old, she was stacking crates of milk bottles by the school gate for collection with two or three of her classmates. Suddenly, a man appeared at the gate and offered the girls money if one of them would go on an errand for him. Instinctively, Nancy knew that he was bad. No one gave you so much money like that. Apart from anything else, he looked different, kind of foreign. He had black, slicked-back hair, high cheek bones and two gold teeth. She told the others not to listen to him, slammed the gate shut and ran to tell the headmistress what had happened, and she rang the police. They discovered that he was a notorious paedophile who was known to the authorities for committing offences against young girls.

From that day on, Nancy's antennae were constantly raised and tuned in to the detection of dangerous men. She always went out in a group because her mother had told her that there was safety in numbers. As time went by, Nancy and her friends knew who all the dirty old men in her district were and just avoided them. They saw them as relatively harmless and pathetic and of no real threat to them as long as they were careful. However, one day, when she was eleven and about to start her first term at high school, she took a neighbour's toddler for a walk in her local park. It was early September and, as her school term started later than some others, there were hardly any people around. The day was warm and sunny and she was wearing a little Aertex blouse and her new school shorts. She was enjoying talking to the child and being in the fresh air. She had only walked a little way into the park, when, from behind a tree just up ahead, stepped the foreign man with the gold teeth; the man from the school gate.

Nancy's heart stopped. Immediately, she swung the pram around and ran into the other part of the park where there was a museum. She thought she would hide in there, where there would be other people. He wouldn't dare to touch her in there. She parked the pram outside, snatched up the boy and climbed up to the first floor. Then she realised that there was absolutely no one around; no noise, no talking, no doors opening and closing. Total silence. And from the window, she could see the man advancing down the path towards the building. Oh, no, he would see the pram. Mustering all her courage, she rushed outside, plonked the child in the pram and ran past him to the road just beyond, without looking at him. He would not try to stop her for fear of being seen. She ran as fast as she could around the perimeter of the park until she reached the safety of her home. She never told her parents what had happened. She could not have foreseen that danger, but she would have to be extra careful in future.

When Nancy was in her early teens, she would go to the park with her friends at the weekends to meet up with others and hopefully to make new friends; boyfriends that is. There, they would often see the same two men. They sat on benches next to each other. Both wore raincoats and held up newspapers in front of themselves. They would look as if they were reading, but as the girls passed, they would whistle and, at the same time, lift up the paper to reveal their exposed members. The girls thought it was hilarious and would run off laughing. And as the men never seemed to leave those benches, they were no threat to them.

However, one day on their usual Sunday trip to the park, another man appeared and Nancy knew instinctively that he was definitely a real danger. He latched on to her gang and followed them around the park trying, like a hyena, somehow to separate one of the girls from the group. He even followed them all the way home and tried to chat with them in the little memorial park near Nancy's house, until her friend's father and brother appeared and threatened him and he shot off on his bike. One thing that Nancy had noticed over time was that men like him often rode Raleigh Rudge bicycles with thick, sit-up-and-beg handlebars and a little round bag on the back of the seat. She kept a eye out for this and often wondered what such men kept in those bags.

About a year later, she discovered just how dangerous this man was. It was a lovely Sunday afternoon and many parents were out with their children in the park, which was divided into two sections. There was the lower part with a bird cage, fountain and formal flower beds and, from there, a set of steep stone steps led up to an area where there was a bandstand and, further on, the museum. Just at the top of these steps was a triangular flower bed with a wide grass border. Lying there on the grass, in broad daylight, with an enormous erection, was the man who had pestered her and her friends. He did not move. Did not seem at all affected by what people said to him. In fact, no one challenged him at all. Fathers seemed more concerned about having the embarrassment of explaining to their children what was happening and so hurried them away from the scene. Nancy was absolutely shocked that no one did anything to stop him, shout at him or hit him for being so depraved. Even at her tender age, she was astounded that he had such a powerful sexual urge that nothing diminished his performance. Perhaps it even stimulated him. He needed to be taken off the streets before some child came to harm, but if grown men would not tackle him then someone would eventually get hurt. Over the years, she often wondered how many young girls he had assaulted and terrified so that their lives were changed forever. Perhaps it was not always girls.

One day, when Nancy was married with children, she went to visit her mother and took the children for a walk in the park of her childhood. To her amazement, the same two raincoated men were sitting on the same two benches reading their newspapers. They whistled as she passed and raised their papers as if in salute. She hurried off laughing out loud. "They are still as harmless as ever," she thought.

Yet, quite often, throughout the years, Nancy would have the same disturbing nightmare. She is in the park and wandering along the terraces above the river. (When she was a child, the public were forbidden to enter that area because the railings had been removed for use in the war effort and it was considered dangerous.) As she walks, she becomes aware that someone is following her. She looks round and sees, to her horror, that it is the Slav from the school gate and the park. She runs ahead and tries to escape from him by crossing a bridge over a ravine with a fast-flowing river way below. The bridge is, in fact, just a tree trunk and it is slippy. She knows that this is a precarious thing to do but she has to get away at all costs. However, when she gets to the other side she is confronted by a rock wall and there is nowhere else to go and the man is coming over the bridge. At this point, she always wakes in a sweat. In such situations, her unfailing instinct is absolutely no protection against these dark, unsettling images which rise up from her subconscious to haunt her and rob her of quiet sleep.

Game Changer

IT was time for a big decision. They were both twenty-eight and there was some hard thinking to do. Caroline and Jez had met at Loughborough University when they were studying Sports Sciences. She was from Derbyshire and he was from south London. At present, Caroline worked in youth services and Jez was a fitness instructor and both were based in London. They had been married a year and wanted to start a family, but life in the city was so expensive that they knew they would never be able to buy a child-friendly home. Apart from anything else, there was climate change and global warming to be taken into account. Did they want to be stuck in an overheated city for the rest of their lives or should they escape and make for the hills? Above all, they desperately wanted a dog. They had to do it now. They both loved the outdoors and spent their weekends running in parks or along towpaths and, now and again, going off to Snowdonia for mountain walking or going rambling in the Peak District. They wanted open spaces and fresh air.

Caroline loved the Peak District; it was her home territory. Her father was a sports teacher and would often take her out on long rambles when she was a child and, if truth be told, she had missed the hills during her years in London; everywhere was so flat. Okay, she loved the buzz and whirl of it all, but you couldn't be going out to bars, cafés and bistros for the rest of your life. Sure, they would miss their friends, but there had to be something more and she was confident that they would make new friends very soon. They had already started to put out feelers for jobs and things looked promising. Indeed, there was plenty of scope for both of them around the Castleton area, so their plan was to rent a cottage for a fortnight and get a feel for the area before deciding whether to take the leap.

Although they had almost decided to make this move, Caroline was not sure that Jez was entirely committed to the idea. He had lived all his life in London, except for the brief spell in Loughborough, and sometimes his friends in the pub would rib him about how his accent would change in no time. They joked that he would soon be saying, "Ee bah gum" and "ecky thump" and they would no longer recognise him. When they said this, Caroline quipped that it was certainly better than saying, "Shat ap", for in the North, 'shat' was considered to be rather a vulgar word to use in company. They laughed at this, but she was serious. The joke was beginning to pall. She had lost count of the number of times she had had to remind people, who rather impolitely commented on the way that she pronounced certain words, that 'butter', 'sugar' and 'Putney' were all spelt with a 'u' and not an 'a'. It was language apartheid, with one particular pronunciation being considered, by some, to be superior.

If Jez was having misgivings about any future children speaking with a northern accent then she felt just as strongly about any children they might have speaking with an Estuary twang, if they stayed in London. She knew that it was an issue to be thought about. To speak in a different way was for her like wearing someone else's clothes. At least one of them was going to feel like a foreigner in another country and, by the same token, any children they had would speak in a different accent from one of their parents. It was a question of identity. For Caroline, however, at the bottom of it all, it really wasn't about the way anyone spoke, it was about space, nature and a better quality of life for all. She hoped that something on this trip might help to persuade Jez. He had only to look at the price of houses for God's sake.

They took a little stone cottage just on the edge of the village of Edale, which was the southern starting point for the Pennine Way and always busy with walkers, whatever time of year. Every day, they would lay out their maps and decide on a walk or wider tour by car. Caroline liked the way the Peak District was divided into two distinct parts. There was the Dark Peak and the White Peak, so called because of the underlying geology. In the northern part, the predominant rock was gritstone and the terrain was harder and walking more strenuous; masculine if you like. The southern part was mainly limestone and the countryside there was softer with rounded hills, wooded dales and footpaths aplenty by the side of meandering rivers; a complete contrast in fact. Today, they planned to go up through the village of Edale, then, opposite the school, they would take the footpath to the left along Kinder Low to Barber Booth. From there, they would go up over Mam Tor then down Winnats Pass to Castleton and make their way back to Edale. The sun was out, but not too hot; a perfect day for walking in the hills.

At the top of the village, they turned on to the footpath to Kinder Low. Alongside this path was the school playing field and it was playtime. The children were running, skipping and gambolling around like lambs. Caroline and Jez laughed.

"What a wonderful place to be child," they exclaimed. "Fancy that being your playground. Air couldn't be any fresher."

As they walked along, two little girls came running along the other side of the wire fence. They were holding hands and one said to the other earnestly, "Will you be my best friend?"

The other girl replied quite seriously, "Oh, yes please."

"Well then, would you like to see my secret den?"

"That clinches it," shouted Jez jubilantly. "Let's do it."

"Only if you will be my best fwend," said Caroline.

Scenes from French Life

THE young child, Sylvie, almost four years old, looked directly at Isabel and asked, *"Est-ce que ton mari est mort?"* ("Is your husband dead?") As she spoke, Isabel was shocked to detect, in those seemingly innocent young eyes, a hint of malice: a desire to shock and inflict hurt on this foreign stranger. Even at her tender age, she had found a weapon with which to challenge the world. Isabel was somewhat taken aback by the boldness of the question. Her husband had dementia and she had come for a brief respite from caring for him to stay with her French friends, whom she had known for forty years, and here was this small child practising her new skill, hoping to cause upset and chaos. She was old before her years. What future awaited her if she put such arts to use on her journey through life? Isabel's immediate fantasy reaction was to shock the assembled company by replying, "No. He is just gone mad." If she did say this, it would absolutely flout the French code of good manners, especially at the dinner table. That was unthinkable if she wished to continue her friendship with the child's grandparents, which she valued.

Here she was in the Languedoc, in this rambling, ten-bedroom, three-storey house sitting in its eight-acre park, where nothing was ever thrown away; where the original art deco wallpaper was peeling off the bedroom walls on the upper floor; where the dining room was full of the car parts of a 1920s wooden car, which had belonged to her friend's father and which she was restoring; where the electricity cables crackled when you switched on a lamp; where the mouse traps were suspiciously larger than normal; and, outside, the trees were encroaching slowly on the house, like Sleeping Beauty's castle. This was more than just shabby chic. It was French provincial life and Isabel loved its quirkiness.

The Mailloux family had come into Isabel's life when their sons became pen friends when they were thirteen; the 'boys' were now in their fifties. The children had not continued with the correspondence, but Isabel had remained firm friends with the parents, Michel and Sandrine. They had welcomed her into their home and, through them, she had been introduced to French family life and its traditions. And over the years, Isabel noticed that the same few words cropped up frequently in conversations: *patrimoine*, *terroir*, *la France profonde* and *l'amour*.

These words seemed to encapsulate the very elements of Frenchness. And Isabel had come to understand what *patrimoine* (inheritance) meant to French people and she knew that it was the reason why Sandrine would never think of selling their lovely old house. She kept the children's bedrooms exactly as they were when the children had gone off to university, hoping that, in the future, her grandchildren would come often to sleep in those same beds. As well as having her own home, Sandrine had also inherited her parents' house, four hundred years old, fifteen bedrooms and a vineyard, and there was absolutely no question of selling it off, no matter what the cost.

It was exactly the same for Michel. His mother, who lived not far from them in the south, kept the house in Normandy where she was born and where Michel had grown up, and she would retreat there from the heat for several months at the height of summer. It was an old, black-and-white *chaumière* (thatched cottage), which had once been the cider-pressing house for the village and Isabel would go to Normandy sometimes to join Sandrine and her family when they were staying there in the summer. Then, there would be many visits from the extended family; uncles, aunts, cousins, children of cousins, all coming to say hello, and then there would be family meals out in the fresh air under the trees.

Michel's bachelor uncle, Dominic, was often there. He owned the manor house in the village close by. And, although he lived in another part of France and rented the manor out, he came periodically to do repairs and meet up with the family and his tenants. One day, after lunch, he offered to take Isabel to see his *manoir*. It had been built in the eighteenth century and stood in its own small park. There was a certain faded beauty about it, but Isabel could imagine what it would have been like in its heyday. In fact, two houses made up the manor. They were mirror images and faced each other across an oval pond brimming with water lilies and flag irises. Leading away from each house was a gravel pathway and at the end of each path, on opposite boundary corners, stood matching gazebos. Like the houses, they looked across to one another. They were miniature, one-room garden houses with beautiful windows and grand fireplaces. They were large enough to dine in, should one be minded to do so.

Dominic opened one of them with an ancient key and, realising that everywhere smelled of damp, immediately lit a fire with twigs and small branches already in the grate. Then, he took down some photograph albums from a cupboard. They were full of studio photos, taken sometime in the 1920s, and were exquisite portraits of his family. There, curling at the edges and fading, were Dominic's parents and siblings. They were a very handsome family and some of the groupings were delightful. It was sad to see such neglect and Isabel felt that these images belonged more properly in a museum, where they could be conserved for people to enjoy an intimate glimpse of a lost era. Instead, they were being left to decay in this mausoleum, at the bottom of a neglected garden. Being the eldest son, Uncle Dominic had inherited all these possessions from his parents, but what price inheritance if you did not have the money or stamina to preserve it? It was so typically French. "If I were a musician," Isabel thought, "I would compose an elegiac sarabande to capture this sense of faded courtly grandeur, of melancholy and nostalgia." She could almost hear it; the past speaking to her.

Land in France is fiercely protected and passed down through the generations. It is their *terroir* and the place where they are firmly rooted. Once, when Isabel was with Michel and Sandrine in Normandy, Michel took her on a tour of his childhood haunts.

"There," he said, pointing to a large house, "is where my grandparents lived and my great-grandmother before that. It has now passed to my cousin."

A little further on he pointed to a farm where Charolais cattle browsed contentedly in rich pastures.

"That farm is where another cousin lives. He inherited from my uncle." And so it went on, with Michel pointing out one place after another that was owned by some member of his family. Isabel realised that it was not a question of showing off wealth or possessions, but it was an expression of his deep love of the land and pride that the family had kept the connection to their land unbroken down through the ages.

On another occasion, when she was visiting them in the south, Michel and Sandrine took her to meet the in-laws of one of their daughters. They lived a little further south than her friends and spoke Occitane, the ancient language of the Pays d'Oc. The husband's mother lived with them. She was one hundred and two, with a mind as sharp as a razor. She had come to the house as a young bride, she told Isabel, and would only leave when her life was over. Over several years, Sandrine's son-in-law and his father had restored all the old buildings in local stone. Between them, when their jobs permitted, they had also made a large vegetable garden and planted fruit trees, so they were almost self-sufficient. They were indeed rooted to their place. For lunch that day they dined on a salad of lettuce, tomato and onion with fried aubergine slices, all home-grown. There was pork terrine made by the mother-in-law from their own pigs. This was followed by locally caught rabbit served with potatoes and peas from the *potager* and the meal was completed with a delicious rhubarb pie. Here indeed was *terroir* exemplified.

Several years later, Isabel was invited to go with Sandrine and Michel to a wedding in a beautiful medieval, hilltop village. The bridegroom was a friend of the Mailloux's son and his bride-to-be was a farmer's daughter, whose family had always owned the land at the bottom of the hill below the village. The reception was to be held in one of the large barns in the farmyard after the ceremony in the ancient church near the top of the hill. The lay priest who officiated was a member of a quasi-religious community to which the bridegroom and his family had once belonged. He was not a fully ordained priest, but could perform marriages and baptisms, which was fortunate because, after the couple had exchanged their vows, he also baptised their baby. "The Catholic church has certainly changed," thought Isabel, somewhat surprised by the modernity of it all. After the ceremony, the guests were invited to take aperitifs in the community's refectory and here was yet another surprise. Some of the order were nuns, who wore brown habits and white wimples, but this lay priest had a wife and so did his colleague, who ran the place with him. "What has happened to tradition?" wondered Isabel. It was really confusing, as she had always regarded France as a thoroughly Catholic country with strict rules about what was or was not permitted.

After the drinks and canapés, the guests made their way down the hill to the farm. The bride and groom had made the bread for the meal, the farmer had made all the wine and a simple, traditional country meal had been prepared. As people began to take their seats, the priest and his colleague arrived with their wives. Isabel was amazed to see that the so-called 'priest' was wearing a very expensive suit and watch and what looked like handmade shoes; Italian probably. The rest of his party were similarly dressed. "What is going on here?" Isabel asked herself, considering that the aim of the order was to help homeless, poverty-stricken people. She questioned Michel about them and he told her that both of the men had been industrial chemists in Switzerland before they founded the community. "Hmmm," thought Isabel. "Some priest then." She noticed that when any of the pretty nuns approached him, the priest would put his arm around their waists and pat their bottoms. Phoney was the only word Isabel could think of.

Local musicians played while people ate and, after the meal, the tables were cleared away and there was dancing; rustic dances that everyone knew. Sandrine danced with some old men who looked as if they had not taken to the floor with a woman for years. She felt sorry for them. Meanwhile, Isabel danced with Michel. She had noticed that, during the course of the evening, the father of the bride had gathered in a corner with his friends. They all wore flat caps, pulled to a point low down on their foreheads. She asked Michel what that was all about. He told her that they represented *la France profonde*. This is what French people called the deepest countryside, where traditions and a way of life have remained unchanged for centuries. In actual fact, he said that they were ultra-right conservatives, chauvinist xenophobes, who were to be given a wide berth.

There was a pause in the dancing and the father of the bride demanded that the musicians play some of the old songs. He and his cronies started to sing. It was not long before Isabel realised that most of the songs were about fighting the English and what filthy, flea-ridden people the English were. "So this is what *la France profonde* actually means. It was not really about deep forests and untouched countryside," she said to herself. "It's about so-called 'priests' hiding in quiet backwaters, getting up to God knows what, and absolute racists pretending they are defending their country and their way of life."

During all the years that Isabel had been going to France, one word above all was used most often, *l'amour*; love of one's mistress, wife, children, family, land – probably in that order. You would think that they had invented it. It made her smile. However, she had to admit that there was a certain attraction in a Frenchman speaking English to you in that delightful accent. One could be seduced even though a flashing light came on above one's head saying 'stereotype'. Michel and Sandrine's youngest daughter had just qualified as a doctor. When she got married, Isabel was invited to the wedding. And, so that Isabel would not feel left out, they asked one of their daughter's friends from medical school to be her escort for the day.

The wedding was held in the local village church and the reception in the Mailloux's garden. There were two hundred guests and the young people had decorated all the tables with sunflowers, gathered illegally from the local fields. It was a beautiful hot day and a wonderfully happy occasion. Isabel enjoyed meeting members of the family she had not seen for ages and getting into conversation with strangers. It was not until it was dark and a little cooler that the meal was actually served and everyone ate by candlelight. Magical. Her companion for the day was Etienne. He was very attractive, attentive and interesting to chat to. They got on extremely well and, while they ate, they talked about their lives. Suddenly, he said to her in the candlelit dark, "And is your husband still active?" Isabel knew exactly what he meant by that question and was somewhat flattered, but was absolutely not going to fall into that trap. "Imagine being seduced by someone half your age and a friend of the family to boot. Imagine," she thought, somewhat wistfully. So she replied, "Well, yes. We go out on long walks and he rides his bike most days." *Vive l'amour à la française*!

This memorable weekend was rounded off with some pretty spectacular fireworks. The morning after the wedding, several guests complained that they had been attacked by wasps in their rooms. The family had been plagued with infestations lately so Michel went to see what he could do. What was needed was for someone to light a fire in the grate to smoke the wasps out up the chimney, whilst he climbed a ladder and dropped a kind of wasp-clearing bomb down the flue from outside. His first attempt did not seem to work, so he dropped another one down and, just as he walked away, the chimney exploded taking part of the gable wall with it. Talk about French provincial life!

Foreign Correspondence

Dear Zainab,

Since we spoke rather heatedly the other day after the lecture on the 'Arab Cultural Renaissance', I have thought a great deal about what you said. So I wanted to commit my thoughts to paper to explain to you exactly how I feel about the problems we discussed.

You accuse me of not really understanding what your culture is actually like and that, although I have Arab friends, these are only Westernised Arabs and therefore I cannot have a proper insight into your world. You ask a great deal. How can I? I have never had, nor ever will have, first-hand knowledge of what it is to be an Arab, a Muslim, or Chinese for that matter. And, by the same token, you will never ever, no matter how long you live or however hard you try, know what it is to be a Catholic brought up in England by an Irish father. I would not expect you to. Neither of us can ever truly know the 'other', but we can, with intelligence and humility, try to learn about and make space for him or her in our minds and in our hearts.

My Arab friends, who reside in the West, live constantly with compromise, which, if truth were told, is the natural state of most living organisms and cultures. These friends have chosen to stay here because they see a better future for themselves; somewhere to earn a viable living, which for them constitutes progress. I would never presume to judge them or condemn them in any way. They themselves know only too well what this compromise has cost them morally, physically and spiritually. They have learnt, by their relocation, that certainties are rare and that life is about making fundamental adjustments and being pragmatic. You are truly blessed if you can live your whole life within a culture where all the answers are given and tradition sustains you completely.

The paradox of modern life is the paradox that has always dogged civilized man. How much change do we accept before we become something else, something we do not want and never intended? The connected, global world makes change inevitable no matter how hard one tries to stem the tide by formulating new laws and preaching fundamentalist ideas. The ancient Greek philosopher, Plato, argued that the aristocratic society was the most ideal type of republic; a society in which everyone had their place and the order remained unchanged and where life was structured and utterly predictable. This is similar to what you have in Islam and I had as a Catholic. Unfortunately, life moves on. Progress is made and change inevitably follows, making reassessment and adjustment necessary. Stasis and change are bound together like Siamese twins and they seem to operate alternately within societies; all societies. A society that does not change and clings *rigidly to its first principles becomes authoritarian, dogmatic and sterile, just as change for the sake of change destroys societies and beliefs. Both routes are dangerous.*

You may hear me going on about the evils and wrongs that I perceive within my own society, and I see its faults, but this does not mean that I want to belong to another culture, or live somewhere else. I can't. I belong here and the best I can do is to work to address the ills within my own society by making myself aware of corruption and malpractice and fighting them when I meet them, by recognising when I am being manipulated for someone else's ends and never accepting injustice. I am the first to admit that the West has behaved badly in many ways, but there are few societies that are not flawed and corrupt in their power base and we should all know this. I love my country. I love my friends with all their faults, but I hate any government that promotes greed and injustice and strips us of our dignity by stealth.

I am taking this course of study because I want to know and understand, to open a window onto a new and wider world. I am not trying to be one of you, as you said. I just want more knowledge, but not in a dilettante way. I might ask why you choose to study aspects of your own culture in a foreign country. You, like me, I presume, are looking for insight and furtherance of knowledge and I would not criticise you for that or deny you the right to do it. We are two different plants, you and I; a cactus and a snowdrop.

If one were to plant the cactus in the cool, damp woods of northern Europe, it would die, for the conditions would be completely hostile for its survival and vice versa for the snowdrop in the searing heat. If, however, you want a rare plant in your environment, you have to make special arrangements for it; build a hot house or a cool house and give it just the right nourishment. It is the same for transplanted cultures, you have to make room for them. Plants flourish best when all the conditions are right, the soil, the air and the light, and so do people. I cannot ask the snowdrop to be a cactus and neither can you.

Written in friendship,

Anne-Marie.

Duende

JENNY and Nick were spending the summer holidays working their way slowly west across northern Spain from the port at Bilbao to Santiago de Compostela in Galicia, planning to arrive there by 25th July for the celebration of the feast of St James. They had been travelling all day in the parching heat and had arrived in the city of Burgos around five in the afternoon. Their first thought was to find a hotel and have a long, cool shower.

Whilst looking for somewhere to park near the cathedral, they discovered to their delight that traffic had been prohibited from circulating in that area while repairs were being made to the facade of the building. This meant that they could park without fear of being fined. As they got out of the car, they noticed a small hotel right next to the cathedral, Hotel Mesón del Cid. Exactly what they were looking for. They booked a room with a balcony which looked out onto the delicately carved buttresses of the ancient building. It could not have turned out better. Many of the streets around had been pedestrianised, so all was peace and tranquillity and they looked forward to a good night's sleep.

As soon as they were washed and refreshed, they set out to explore Burgos. It was beautiful. They discovered an elegant tree-lined walk along by the river, outside the city walls, and the good burghers of Burgos were making full use of it in the early evening. Jenny and Nick joined with them in their *paseo*, the stroll that Spaniards love to take before their evening meal. They received and gave greetings to passers-by as they walked along. "*Buenas tardes, Señor y Señora.*" It was so human and genial and they loved the ritual of it all. And, as the evening cooled a little, their thoughts turned to food.

Just by a gate in the city walls, they found a small family restaurant where they knew they would find good home-cooked food, and they were not disappointed. The rice pudding was delicious. During the evening, they struck up a conversation with two French couples who were walking the Camino de Santiago and Nick was interested to find out how difficult it was, as it was something he had always wanted to do. It was a exciting, international evening and they strolled back to their hotel feeling pleased with their day and ready for bed in crisp white sheets.

However, their day was not quite over. As they tried to get off to sleep around midnight, they became aware of a commotion in the square outside. They opened the shutters and found that three young gypsy lads had collared a group of blond Scandinavians and made them sit down on the cathedral steps. At first, Jenny and Nick could not make out what was happening. Were the tourists being attacked or threatened in some way? Then all became clear as they watched the spectacle unfold. The eldest boy, about ten years old, seemed to be reciting the story of El Cid, that famous Spanish hero, adopted son of Burgos. He emphasised his role by much strutting up and down and swinging of his makeshift sword, while he declaimed the legend of that celebrated warrior. When he had finished his story, the other two boys began singing flamenco songs, with all the harshness and sorrow of their gypsy ancestors. They sang and danced unselfconsciously as their forebears had done for centuries before. An older man appeared to tell them to come away, but they ignored him and kept on keening and clapping as if driven by an ancient spirit. As the boys sang, they seemed to Jenny and Nick to embody their tribe's grief; body and soul were fused with the old songs, which were freighted with history's tears. It was raw, visceral and profoundly moving. This was surely *duende*.

Hobson's Choice

I DON'T know what I'm doing here really and I don't think I like it. I want to go home to my nice little house. Me and Noel moved in there the day we got married and I have never lived anywhere else. Or wanted to, for that matter. But, our Pauline thought that it would be better for everyone if I came here for a rest. Better for who I'd like to know? Not for me. She keeps telling me that I've been having lots of falls lately but I don't know about that. Perhaps she's just making it up to get shut of me. She says that I keep forgetting to take my tablets, but I say that everybody can forget things. I bet she does. All the time, probably. She says that when I forget my tablets it makes me ill and they have to call the ambulance. Well, I think she's making that up. I've never been in an ambulance in my life. She always pestering me about this and that, so I tell her that I feel a bit faint and then she goes away while I have a little nap. That's one way of stopping her chatter.

If I don't like it here, I'll get Noel to take me home, but our Pauline keeps saying that he can't come just yet. He's got a bad leg. Besides, she says, there is someone else living in our house now. Well, Noel will soon sort them out. Cheeky beggars.

A new woman has just come to stay here and she looks like trouble. She keeps banging her cup down on the table to get the nurses to go over and see to her. When I get over there, I'll give her a clout round the ear. That should stop her once and for all. I know, I'll take that blasted cup off her. That'll stop her game. Serve her right. Who does she think she is?

Every day there seem to be different people working here. They come in and out, in and out and they change all the time. It's very confusing. I can't make head nor tail of it all. Some days there are nice people. They comb your hair. Do your nails. I like that big, fat, jolly one. She's got a right lovely smile and nothing's too much trouble. "Come on, Win," she says. "Let's get you dolled up. Your Pauline'll be here soon. Can't have you looking like the *Wreck of the Hesperus.*" She makes me laugh. I don't like the one who seems to be in charge, though. She swans around like a queen, but she never seems to do any work. She just looks about and gives orders. If I was her boss, I'd give her a mop and bucket and see how she'd like that.

Dear me, they are so blooming noisy in here. Some people make strange sounds all the time; the same sound over and over again. It's driving me mad. The man in the corner, over there, he makes the most noise and it goes on all day. I can't get any peace. I tell him to shut up. Stupid old fool. Honestly, some folk don't half annoy you. If I was his wife, he'd soon hear from me. My Noel wouldn't go on like that. Where is he anyway? Perhaps he doesn't know I am here. I'd better get home soon or he'll be worrying.

There are some new nurses now, boys as well as girls. Lovely black hair, nice dark eyes and smooth brown skin. They are kinder than some of the others and, at night sometimes, when I can't sleep, they stroke my hand and talk to me about Noel and Pauline. It's nice that. Where is our Pauline, anyway? She's not been for ages. I need her to get me out of here. Can't be sitting round all day talking to these people. Jobs need doing at home and Noel never seems to do it right for me. Got to be watching him all the time.

Then there's the music. Bang, bang, bang, jangle, jangle, bump. What's that all about? It's just a load of noise. Them young nurses seem to like it though. Perhaps when it's loud they can't hear people shouting for them. That suits them, I'm sure. Our Pauline will put me something nice on when she gets here. She knows how to switch the wireless over.

A nice man has come to stay here now. Charlie, I think his name is. Anyway that's what our Pauline said, but I forget people's names as soon as they tell me. He sits in the armchair next to me and nods and smiles when I look over. He seems to like the music our Pauline puts on for us and I notice that he sometimes taps his feet and fingers when the music is playing. Sometimes, though, the girls switch it over just when we are enjoying it. It's the same with the telly. Anyhow, he doesn't make funny noises like that other bloke. He just sits there quietly. Never see anyone coming to visit him. Funny that. Where's his wife?

Our Pauline was here a minute ago. She's gone to have a word downstairs because things aren't quite right. Something to do with my clothes being all over the wardrobe floor instead of on the hangers. But, if our Pauline has gone to have words, someone will be in for it. Don't know what she's making a fuss about though. She's always getting on her high horse about something.

I wonder when my Mum and Dad will be coming to see me. They must know I am in hospital. Our Pauline says they are away on holiday. Well, they need to get their backsides over here. I want to go home and see our dog, Florrie.

A new lad's started working here. Lovely black curly hair like our Pauline's lad. He's just come in and said he's going to take me for a walk in the garden. That's good of him. He doesn't need to do it really, but he said he likes doing it, likes my company. I remind him of his Gran, he says.

My God, there was a woman sitting in my chair when we came back from the garden. She won't move. When anyone tries to get her out of the chair, she screeches like a banshee. Wants a good smack. She goes on all the time about some dead children and God Almighty. I'll give her God Almighty if she doesn't get out of my chair. Can't someone please shut her up?

The nice man who sits next to me has started to make funny noises now. It's a sort of choking sound like a hoarse cough as if there is something stuck in his throat. He was shouting for someone to help him, but they all seem busy. They don't seem worried. Just keeping walking past him and chatting to each other. It doesn't seem right to me. He's such a lovely chap. I'll get someone when they come past. Oh, our Pauline has just walked in. She'll sort it.

The nurses have taken him to his bed. Hope his cough gets better soon.

When I was at the breakfast table just now, Charlie was there but he wasn't eating anything. He just kept making those awful sounds. Nobody took any notice of him even though he was calling out for help. How can they not see that things aren't right? Some of these girls are real lazy buggers. You could starve or be at death's door and they wouldn't notice.

Our Pauline has just been in. She was very, very angry, more than I have ever seen her before. She told me that Charlie, the nice man, died yesterday. She was going to see about it. "Heads will roll for this," she said. And I am sure they will, if she has anything to do with it.

A Touch of Magic

ROSEMARY was six when some boys at school told her that Father Christmas did not exist. She cried all the way home. Something precious had been stolen from her. It wasn't so much the Father Christmas thing; she had begun to suspect that whole story anyway. It was the magic of it all that the boys had spoiled for her. For just a few days in the year everything seemed possible. If He could exist, then why not fairies, elves, pixies and even wicked witches? She so much wanted there to be more; more than she could see around her in her everyday life.

After that day, she found that she was always quietly on the lookout for the extraordinary; incidents and events that were inexplicable but had something indefinable, yet true, about them. She would sit quietly in a corner and listen to the grown-ups talking and she would find meaning in something such as two people saying exactly the same thing at the same moment. What made them do that? There must be some silent connection between their brains. But what was it? Most of all she loved to climb up on her Dad's knee and listen to stories about his childhood, especially the ones that had a certain magical, mysterious element in them.

One of her favourites was about the time when his mother sent him to collect the hens' eggs from the hedgerow. There, he found a clutch of three, all white, and on each one was a fingerprint in blood. She knew he was telling the truth because he wasn't the sort of person to tell lies. But who or what spirit had left those marks? Why hadn't they just stolen the eggs? Was it a sign of something? It sent shivers down her spine. But the most fascinating and inexplicable tale by far was the one about some dreams he had had when he was about twelve and ill in bed with a high fever.

For three consecutive nights, Rosemary's father dreamt that their white horse had escaped from the field and had gone down to the lake. He was frightened that the horse might drown, get into danger or become lost. So, in reality and still sleeping, he got out of bed and went out to search for the horse. His mother would find him outside in his wet night clothes and bring him back to the house. On the fourth morning, they found the horse dead by the lake. As far as Rosemary was concerned, this simply had to mean something. Surely her father's dreams had foretold of the death of the horse? What was the connection between her father and the horse? There must be some explanation. At her young age, she didn't have the words or concepts to express what she thought about it all, but she felt that there must be another part of the world that humans could not understand or see. There had to be or why would these things happen? She had heard some of her parents' friends talk about second sight. Now, what did that mean? Was it connected to this whole thing that she was trying to understand?

When she was twenty-one, Rosemary married and moved away from her home town. Her life was busy and for many years she had not thought about those unexplained things that had so caught her imagination as a child. However, one day her father was reminiscing about the old times, talking about courting her mother and how he had enjoyed their wedding day. Then he told her about something that had happened to him about ten years after their marriage. He was sent away on a job for a few days to an area where the best man from his wedding lived and thought it would be nice to catch up. His friend was delighted to see him and invited him in. But her father apologised to him and said that he had obviously come on the wrong day.

"What on earth do you mean?" his friend asked him. Her father replied, "Well, I have just seen your daughter at the top of the stairs wearing a first communion dress so you must be really busy."

"You had better come in," said his friend. They sat down and he told Rosemary's father that his daughter had died several years ago on her first communion day. Her father had no idea of this tragic event as they had been out of touch for a while. He was terribly shocked.

Rosemary wondered why her father had never told her about this. Perhaps he was a little frightened of this power; this gift which had been bestowed on him. Maybe he felt that people would not believe him or even think that he was somehow a little strange in the head. She was sure he was not. For whatever reason, her father had some kind of connection, of knowledge of that other level of being, of altered consciousness, and she would explore this idea further. She would read whatever she could find on the subject. There had to be something in it, for her father seemed to have been chosen in some way, like a channel or conduit. She couldn't really express it. For example, on her parents' wedding day, three couples were married in the church and each couple married someone with the same surname. "Now, how often does that happen?" Rosemary asked herself. Then, when her parents arrived at the place where they were staying for their honeymoon, they could not sleep because someone was playing music outside. They looked out to see a huge harvest moon sitting almost on the horizon and a gypsy wedding party celebrating on the village green. For Rosemary that combination was pure magic and quite out of the ordinary.

Indeed, something happened to Rosemary herself one day that convinced her that unseen forces were at work. She had gone to a university summer school in London and met a woman on the first day who, finding out where she came from, asked if she could possibly have lift back home at the end of the week, as, coincidentally, they lived very near to each other. During that week of intensive study, Rosemary attended some thought-provoking lectures on philosophy given by an Anglican canon and, at the end of the course, she went to look for him to say how much she had enjoyed his lectures. As she approached the lecture hall, she said to herself, "If there is anything at all in these mysterious happenings, he will be here." She entered the lecture hall and, lo and behold, he was standing there in the empty room.

"Oh," she said. "I just came to thank you for your enlightening lectures."

He said, "Thank you, my dear, but you don't need enlightenment, you just need more light." Rosemary was stunned. It was one of those moments.

She left the hall and went to pick up her companion for the journey home. It was a bad time to be leaving London;

four-thirty on a Friday afternoon. The traffic moved slowly; stop, start, stop, start every few minutes. The woman asked Rosemary about her job and she, in turn, asked her what she did.

"I am a clairvoyant," said the woman, "and your life at the moment is a bit like this motorway, a little forward and then a stop. You are not sure which way to go." And that was certainly true. Rosemary had reached a point in her life when she had some major decisions to make which would affect her future. She had to get it right. Then the woman continued, "What you need right now is enlightenment." Rosemary could not believe what she was hearing. Two people, two complete strangers, had both used the same word, out of all the words in the world, in the last hour. She was absolutely flabbergasted. Now she was certain that there was magic, or whatever you might call it, in the world.

So, over time Rosemary read everything she could lay her hands on. She read books on spiritualism, supernatural events like out-of-the-body experiences, even a little on UFOs, but that was too science-fiction for her and, in any case, what had aliens got to do with what she wanted to understand? While she was researching all these various avenues, she came upon an engraving which perfectly encapsulated what she was trying to discover. It was a medieval wood engraving by an unknown artist and depicted a philosopher breaking through the membrane of the planet Earth to discover the worlds beyond it. That was just it. Exactly.

In recent years, she had become extremely interested in certain areas of science which she thought might hold a key to the mystery. There was the Many-Worlds theory of quantum mechanics, for example, which stated that it was possible for multiple realities to coexist. That was an interesting avenue for further research. Then there was the Dark Matter theory. Scientists had proved that it existed because of its apparent effects on the world around, but because it did not emit light, it could not be detected. What if the mystery lay there? However, the area that Rosemary was most drawn to was that of Magnetic Fields. Recently, scientists had shown how birds were able to fly huge distances across the oceans from their nesting sites to over-wintering sites in different continents and land in exactly the same location when they arrived at each site. They had discovered that the birds do this by following the earth's magnetic field which they can detect with an area of their brain, or more precisely their eyes. Rosemary had also learned, in her reading, that trees communicate and actually help each other through a vast network of connected root systems. Speech was not necessary but connectedness certainly was. So perhaps, thought Rosemary, some explanation of the mysteries that had always intrigued her lay in an amalgam of all these theories. But what if she found the answers she was searching for? Wouldn't the magic disappear? She didn't know if that's what she really wanted.

She did not often talk to her friends about these matters for fear of their scornful reactions. When she did, some were quite scathing, telling her that belief in such things was nonsense and there was only what you could actually see in the real world. Others thought she was just a little weird. But one day, Rosemary attended the funeral of a very good friend who was in her nineties. They had become close friends years ago, even though there was a thirty-year age gap between them. They had been attracted to each other through a mutual love of literature and gardening. After the ceremony, family and friends met up outside the chapel. It was a very still, warm spring day but suddenly a fierce wind got up, a mini-whirlwind in fact, sending caps and hats flying and causing ladies' hair to be blown about and whipped across their faces. And just as suddenly, it died down. Rosemary knew, without a doubt, that it was her friend, Evelyn, bidding her goodbye.

"Goodbye, my beautiful friend," whispered Rosemary and she smiled.

The Jolly Buccaneers

I WENT to stay with a friend in the south for a few days and, on the Saturday, she took me to a small country town that she had never visited before, thinking it would be a good day out for both of us. We parked the car in a small side street, lined with charming brick-built cottages. As we were gathering our belongings, two young boys about ten years old, came down the street. They seemed to be a couple of likely lads, but nice, so I said to them jokingly, "Are you two looking for trouble?"

"Yeah, we are miss," they said cheekily and skipped off, knocking on several windows as they passed. One boy was a pleasant, slim lad with fair hair. The other, obviously his best pal, had the most iridescent green eyes I have ever seen, beautifully set in the loveliest face. He had a shock of unruly hair the colour of lightly toasted wheat, if there is such a colour, a heart-breaker in the making. Cupid would definitely cause him some trouble later, if he hadn't already.

After sauntering around the attractive little town for a while, we began our usual quest for a coffee shop. Eventually we asked a passer-by where he could recommend and he pointed down the street to one facing the zebra crossing where, he said, we could get the best coffee in the county, not to mention the cakes. We found ourselves a comfortable table by the window so we could people-watch, and settled down for a good chat.

It was a little while before we realised what we were watching. Across the road, at the other side of the zebra crossing, was a small supermarket and the two boys were hanging around outside the entrance. Was this somehow connected with their 'looking for trouble'? We sincerely hoped not. Or were they simply waiting to meet up with school pals? So we observed them. To our amazement, we saw that they were helping people, looking for opportunities to assist them. If an old gentleman or lady came out with heavy bags, they would offer to carry them. Now and again, someone in a wheelchair would come up to the crossing and they would offer to see them across the road. The 'beautiful one' had a lovely way with disabled people. He seemed to know exactly what would be of help and they saw people laughing with him as they crossed the road. His friend was good with those who seemed frightened or unsure of their step. It was like a ballet and so heart-warming. And we noticed that silver coins were often proffered in thanks. What a fantastic way to make some pocket money and how unexpected. Ten year old boys were usually little monsters.

As we sat there watching, we discussed the boys and came to the conclusion that they were from happy homes, where the parents had planted good moral compasses in their kids. We made up life stories for them. The quieter blond boy's parents were probably teachers or social workers, something in the caring professions, and he perhaps had sisters rather than stroppy brothers, who would always be wanting to fight with him. The other boy was slightly different. We could imagine his mother; a single parent with just the one child from a failed relationship, slightly hippy and alternative, but very warm and loving. She would be something like an art therapist working with disadvantaged kids or running a youth club. That was the best thing about people-watching, you could fantasise all day long. Even so, there was something really attractive, memorable and genuine about those two young lads.

When we had exhausted the delights of the town, it was time to head back home. As we were walking down the street to the car, the boys were coming up the hill towards us.

"Well, did you find trouble, then?" I asked.

"Yeah, we certainly did, miss," said the one with the eyes. "Lots of it. Have a lovely day." And the jolly buccaneers swaggered off, their pockets bursting with the bounty they had extracted from the passing ships.

Eye of the Beholder

ONE day after school, when Maria was a young girl of about ten, she was waiting for the bus at the stop between the newspaper office and the wallpaper and decorator's shop, when she noticed a brass plaque on the wall which said 'Art Gallery - First Floor'. So she went to see what it was all about. There was no one around, no admission fee to pay. She was free to wander and look. It was like an Aladdin's cave. There were big pictures and small paintings in lovely gold frames and some statues on pedestals. In that moment, she knew that she had made a discovery. In future, it would be her secret place. She wouldn't tell the others about it, but would come as often as she could to look at these things.

Some of the pictures did not appeal to her. People didn't really look like that. They were out of shape and weird. Not at all pretty to look at. She didn't really know what to think about these things and felt a little stupid because she didn't understand the art that was in front of her. Perhaps it was something only for grown-ups and when she was older she would know better, and she certainly wanted to know. But, nevertheless, she had a feeling inside that all of this was special for her somehow and important.

The pieces had little labels beside them saying who painted them and what materials the artist had used. Maria especially liked the oil paintings. In a way, the thick paint made the pictures more vivid and alive. It was amazing what someone could do with just paint and a brush. Artists were clever people. As she wandered about, she came to a section labelled 'Still Life'. "That's a strange thing to call life," thought Maria, but she was entranced by these smaller paintings. You could almost touch that fruit, smell those flowers, feel that fabric, lift that glass. She wished she could do that. It was so beautiful. Better than the real thing almost.

Maria had never been to an art gallery before. She had noticed the big one in the town, near the school dentist's surgery, but she had never been inside it. She supposed that her parents did not think she would be interested. Besides they were busy people and probably thought that she was too young for such things. However, her mother loved pictures. In fact, she would save money from the housekeeping fund to buy them. They were not originals or great works of art, but prints of attractive scenes. There was one that Maria particularly liked. It was of an English thatched cottage set in a cottage garden of hollyhocks, lupins and roses and in one corner was written a little verse:-

Life's treasures are not far afield
Upon some distant shore,
But jewels of peace and happiness
Are found right at our door.

The picture gave her a warm feeling and she would stand in front of it when the house was quiet and drink in its loveliness. It gave her a sense of security and secret happiness, for the words were true. Her mother's favourite was a portrait of a Victorian lady sitting serenely in her drawing room with light striking her from one side. Mum liked it because it reminded her of their own room which, in the late afternoon sun, was flooded with brilliant light just like the picture. The artist had captured the same feeling that she had when she sat there in the early evening, just like that lady.

Maria was about fourteen when her sister won a prize at school. It was a book about the paintings of Vermeer and she was allowed to borrow it. How she loved those portraits, those interiors; the colours, the light, the sense of suspended animation. People were captured in frozen moments, like the young woman by a window reading a letter. It was like a photograph but much more beautiful. Breaths seemed to be held just for an instant and she could imagine life then going on afterwards. The artist had captured it all. He even painted himself in his studio. It was wonderful. After she had discovered Vermeer, Maria set out to find out who had painted what. She wanted to become knowledgeable about art, to be able to recognise the work of the great masters, in case anyone should ask her about the subject in future. Moreover, she wanted to be stunned by beauty in her quest.

So she went to the library and borrowed book after book starting from the Renaissance painters, like Botticelli, and working up to the modern artists. Initially, it was just a question of making lists and notes so she would know in which slot to place an artist. She didn't like all the paintings, especially the great overpowering, historical and mythological ones. She could appreciate their structure, use of colour and play of light, but they did not speak to her. It was storytelling on a grand scale; a bit like a long, dry sermon from the pulpit. She was being instructed by the artist as a passive viewer. Her emotions were not involved. These were not for Maria. They left her cold.

So Maria pursued her quest and suddenly, when she reached the Impressionists, she found that the artists were speaking to her. She understood what they were saying, what they wanted her to feel. She wasn't lost any more in a world she didn't recognise. Some of the paintings were just simple scenes; poplars by Sisley, a snowy lane by Monet, a nude in the bath by Bonnard. Everything was familiar and yet transformed by marvellous light. She particularly loved the paintings by Seurat, 'Bathers at Asnières' and 'A Sunday Afternoon on the Island of La Grande Jatte', because they were done in a different style from some of the other Impressionist painters. The artist had experimented with a style which was called *pointillism* and she thought that it gave the paintings a kind of stillness, indeed, a timelessness, which was so appealing. There were so many paintings that she loved and which gave her deep satisfaction. Sometimes, she did not understand why she found certain ones attractive, but the memory of them stayed with her, enriched her in some way. She was so glad that she had discovered these treasures when she was young and hoped there would be many years before her in which to find many more.

As she grew older, Maria realised that she had been concentrating on oil paintings as if that were the only kind of art there was, but one day she saw a water colour by John Sell Cotman. It was just a simple sketch of water and rocks, and she was hooked. She loved the delicacy of it and the fineness that could be achieved with the medium. Over the years, her list of the water colourists whose work she loved grew. There was Edward Bawden, Eric Ravilious and Paul Nash to name but a few. They were all quintessentially English painters and she loved the spareness and seeming fragility of their work. More than anything, she admired their ability to capture the feeling of the English countryside; of Englishness in fact. There was a gentle tranquillity about their work which drew her to those artists as kindred souls.

But why should this be so? She often pondered that question. How could strokes on canvas or paper have the power to move us, even transform us? And over time, she came to the conclusion that, as humans, we needed to copy what we saw out there in the external world, *mimesis* scholars called it, in order to make our lives real, but, more importantly, to real-ise ourselves. In all its forms, art was the mirror in which we could see our reflection. Without it, we could not know who we really were. Thus we are always creating mirrors, and always have done so since the first cave paintings, in order to give meaning to our lives. In this way, we learn where to place our feet for the next step. We learn how to decorate our surroundings and, most importantly, how to communicate with our fellow man, to love him or at least understand him. We learn how to touch those other faces in that mirror. This strange paradox of the unreal creating the real is what makes us different from other species and it is a great gift. Maria felt that it was a miracle that Man had discovered this phenomenon at all and how it was so very central to our existence. Indeed, George Steiner, the philosopher and polymath, perfectly described how she felt about the power of art:-

Again the shorthand image is that of an Annunciation, of a 'terrible beauty' or gravity breaking into the house of our cautionary being.

If we have heard rightly, the wing-beat and the provocation of that visit, the house is no longer habitable in quite the same way. A mastering intrusion has shifted the light.[*]

One day, she was sitting in the National Gallery in front of a painting by a Dutch master. It was a simple scene of a full dyke beside a lane and bare trees were etched against a February sky. Suddenly and unexpectedly, she found herself in floods of tears. The only explanation she could think of as to why that painting had moved her so deeply was that it displayed the truth of the thing. The artist, by his talent and understanding, had revealed the layer below the surface of life and that was the true purpose of art. At last, she had found what she had been seeking for all this time; beauty in truth, truth in beauty.

---

[*] This quote is taken from George Steiner's book *Real Presences*, p. 143, Faber and Faber Limited. Paperback edition. 1991. ISBN 0-571-16356-4.

Notes on Love

HELENA Molyneux studied Art History and Italian at Exeter University, during which time she spent six months studying Italian in Milan, a city with which she fell in love. When the holidays came round, she liked to go inter-railing around Europe with a group of friends. They travelled mainly to France, Italy and Spain, and undertook long walking tours in high mountain country. It was on one of these trips, in her final year, that she met Greg Laidlaw, a post-grad geology student from Oxford University. She was trekking with two friends and a guide in the Moroccan High Atlas region when she came across him in a small café in the Berber village of Aït Zitoun.

The café was crowded and Greg stood up to offer her his seat, speaking to her in Spanish. With her long dark hair, brown eyes and golden-brown skin, coupled with Morocco's proximity to the Spanish mainland, he presumed she must be Spanish. He was surprised to find, when she thanked him, that she was actually English. They laughed and he apologised for the mistake. She, in turn, discovered that he was Scottish. In fact, he was a typical Scot with reddish hair, blue eyes, and pale skin; the opposite of Helena.

They got into conversation and he explained what he was doing in the mountains. He was on a field trip, working on a project for his doctorate, which involved tracking down locations where a certain rare rock was to be found, in order to understand the geological history of the planet better and disprove certain current theories. It seemed that this particular rock was only to be found at high altitudes in certain mountain ranges. She liked his enthusiasm for his subject and told him how she, too, loved the high mountains; the clear air, the feeling of being above it all. He asked her what she was studying and what she intended to do when she had finished. Ideally, she told him, she wanted to work with illuminated manuscripts or just old manuscripts in general. She loved the details of everyday life one could glean from some of the illuminations and marvelled at the complicated lettering and the script of these old papers. She also loved the feel of the vellum or parchment which had been used. But she had not yet fixed on any particular branch. It would largely depend on her degree in the end and what was out there for her.

As she was leaving the café, he gave her his phone number saying it would be nice to meet up again should she find herself anywhere near Oxford. She liked him and said that would be a nice idea, so she gave him her number too. She might even be able to persuade him to take her on one of his trips into the mountains. That was something to think about. After that, they were in regular contact. She would go to Oxford and enjoy the libraries and museums there. He would travel down to Exeter and they would walk the coastal paths of Devon and Cornwall, but more importantly for Helena, he did actually invite her to join him several times on his trips to the French Alps and the mountain ranges of North Africa.

After she gained her degree, she found a job working with old manuscripts in the Art History department of the university, which she enjoyed very much. In the meantime, her affair with Greg had become quite serious and he wanted her to move in with him in Oxford. He had gained his doctorate and had been asked to stay on as a junior lecturer in Exeter College. The idea appealed to her so, with Greg's help, she secured a job at the Bodleian Library, doing much the same thing as she was already doing; cataloguing and referencing manuscripts. They rented a small house not far from the university and she took quickly to life in academe. About eighteen months later, they married at a simple ceremony in the Oxford Registry Office. Two and a half years later, she gave birth to twins, Roger and Susan, who inherited their father's red hair and blue eyes. She was outnumbered. No one in her family looked like her.

As time went on, Greg moved up the university hierarchy, eventually being offered a chair in geology and so became Professor Laidlaw. Meanwhile, after a brief break when the children were young, Helena carried on with her work at the Bodleian Library, eventually becoming responsible for the care of some precious acquisitions; rare illuminated folios from the early quattrocento period. And, over the years, her relationship with Greg changed subtly. She watched, with some regret, as he became rather pompous and self-satisfied, pleased with his position at the top of his tree and seduced by collegiate life and all its perks. Helena noticed that he liked to be regarded as the fount of wisdom by his students and there were some post-graduate students, mostly women, who gathered closely around him; campus followers, as one might say. Among these was a young Swiss girl called Heidi

Brunner. She was a mineralogist and worshipped at Greg's feet. She was blonde and wore her fair hair, stereotypically, in plaits around her head; just like the 'real' Heidi of fiction, thought Helena, rather wickedly, on the brief times that she had met her. She was as fresh and wholesome as an Alpine meadow in spring, with a solid peasant figure and sturdy legs perfectly adapted to scaling the mountain crags. In fact, Helena's considered opinion was that she suited Greg in her stolidity.

Just before his fifty-eighth birthday, Greg went off on one of his usual field trips, this time to the French Alps. He hadn't been gone more than four days when Helena received a call from the police. Greg had been killed in a rock fall near l'Alpe d'Huez and the informant of the accident was a Fraulein Heidi Brunner. It turned out there had been no actual field trip, but instead just a holiday *à deux*. Helena was not really surprised about that. She had known that Heidi carried a torch for Greg and had observed how he had enjoyed her unquestioning adoration, but also how he had benefited academically from her expertise and collaboration. Helena realised just how far she and Greg had drifted apart in the past ten years. Nevertheless, she was sorry that she had not had time to say a proper goodbye.

After the funeral, Helena's children, Roger and Susan, began to badger her about what she was going to do now. She slightly resented this as they certainly had never shown any real interest in what she did. They were too much like their father; matter-of-fact and pragmatic, without a romantic bone in their bodies. Along with him, they held the belief that the sciences were far superior to the arts and somehow they looked down on Helena, who spent her life 'fussing', as they put it, with old manuscripts. So, she had to admit to herself that she really did not have much in common with her offspring and had often been made to feel like an outsider in her own home. Roger had studied Economics at LSE and worked in derivatives in the London Stock Market. Susan, who had graduated from Cambridge with a degree in Maths and Statistics, was now employed by an international data management company and worked in central London. They were both doing rather well and had very comfortable lives with their respective spouses and they had one child apiece. Whenever the twins spoke to her about her future plans, Helena got the distinct impression that the conversation was actually about money rather than her well-being.

When Greg died, she inherited quite a large sum. The bulk of this was made up of an inheritance that had come down from his father, which Helena and Greg had invested as their 'rainy day' fund and for their retirement. Fortunately, they had not needed to touch any of it. It now seemed to Helena that the twins thought that some of it was theirs by rights, to be shared equally with her. She absolutely refused to discuss it with them as she did not consider it their business. In the meantime, they could wonder and plot. She continued to work at the Bodleian, sold the large family house and rented a two-bedroom terraced house in a nice part of town, while her plans slowly evolved.

This time, she was going to choose a life which suited her, satisfied her, allowed her to be who she really was. So she asked herself when and where had she been the happiest in all her life? It was working with the manuscripts, delighting in their beauty, unlocking the secrets of the past and gaining insight into lives lived long ago; almost hearing the dead speak, as it were. That had satisfied her. And now she saw it all plainly for the first time. She was paper; her illuminated manuscripts. Greg was stone; his rocks and minerals. Stone was hard, immovable, and it was difficult to leave traces on it. Whereas, paper was soft, malleable, and ciphers could easily be traced upon its surface. You could be wrapped in paper, enveloped. Not so with stone. Thinking of these differences, she was reminded of the Cuban film, *The Elephant and the Bicycle* and the scenes with the blind schoolmistress, Doña Iluminada. Before the socialist revolution, she would ask the pupils to look up at the clouds and describe to her what they saw. Some said they could see elephants. Others could see bicycles. They were using their creative imagination and anything was possible. After the revolution, the teacher regained her sight and when she asked the children what they saw when they looked at the clouds, they replied factually and statistically with reports of what kind of clouds they were, at what altitude they were and what weather they were predicting. In fact, the magic had disappeared and that is how Helena had felt for years.

She loved speaking Italian and had adored living in Milan. So she made up her mind that she would go back there. She would revert to being Helena Molyneux and start afresh. Be open to new sights and feelings. Live more fully. She was fifty-seven and the children tried to persuade her that it was a bad time in life to be branching out, but Helena was determined. It had to be done now or never. With good references from the Bodleian, she secured a post at the Biblioteca Ambrosiana; a library founded in 1607 by Cardinal Borromeo, and said her goodbyes to family and friends. So three years after Greg's death, she was to be found living in a small one-bedroom apartment not many streets away from the library where she worked and within easy reach of the magnificent cathedral and the exquisite Galleria Vittorio Emanuele II, with its attractive shops and cafés. It was a dream come true.

Helena immersed herself in her work. The library was amazing. There was so much to see and enjoy and the collections were fantastic. She loved the antiquity of the building and the smell of old leather. She soon made friends who invited her to cafés for lunch or to have meals with their families. It was as if she had finally come home. About a year after she started working there, the library received a bequest from a wealthy art collector. It consisted of old manuscripts; some illuminated and many other documents relating to purchases he had made over the decades. Helena was entrusted with the job of examining and cataloguing them and assessing their historical importance. It was extremely rewarding work.

One day, there was a knock on her office door and a man walked in.

"Excuse me," he said. "I am looking for Madame Molyneux." He pronounced her name with a slight French twist as he said it in Italian.

She laughed and said, "You have found her."

"Oh," he said, surprised. "I thought I was looking for a French lady, but I have found an English one instead. I apologise, but I thought that it couldn't possibly be you because you look Italian. What a delightful confusion. Three countries in just a few moments."

"A delightful confusion, indeed," thought Helena. She liked his quirky humour. He was taller than the average

Italian, with dark wavy hair, greying at the temples, and had a spare, loose frame that suggested to Helena that he was a mountain walker. He looked about sixty years old, probably a few years older than her; altogether an attractive man, she thought.

"Excuse me," he said. "Please let me introduce myself. I am Emilio Affini, an art historian. I work at the Pinacoteca del Castello Sforzesco and my work involves authenticating paintings and establishing provenance for disputed pieces. I know that a bequest has recently come into your library's possession from the noted collector Alfonso de Luca, and I have reason to believe that among those papers there may be some documents which will help me to establish the authenticity of one particular painting in our gallery."

"Well, I have only just begun the painstaking task of finding out exactly what we have. It will take some time," said Helena. "However, if you leave me all the details and your number, I will let you know if I find anything of interest to you."

"That is most kind of you," said Emilio. "I look forward to hearing from you." He shook her hand and bowed slightly as he did so. She loved the mannerliness of that gesture. It was so long since she had experienced that level of courteous behaviour. It pleased her greatly.

Over the following months, Helena came across several documents which she thought might be of interest to Emilio. She would telephone him and he would come over to the library or he would invite her to meet him at some café in the Galleria that he thought she might like. They both enjoyed these meetings and, as the months went by, there were more invitations to dinner, to the theatre, to galleries and for trips into the mountains for walking or simply to take in the beauty of the landscape. Emilio loved the way Helena looked. He asked her where her dark looks came from but she honestly could not tell him. She had always been told that she looked like her grandmother, but apart from that no one knew from whom she had inherited her dark complexion. Indeed, her father often laughingly called her his genetic throw-back because she looked nothing like her parents. She was handsome rather than beautiful, with strong features and a slim figure, which she showed off by the simple but classic clothes she wore. She had a flare for style and colour and Emilio was pleased and proud to be in her company. During the time they spent together, they talked about their lives and she discovered that he was a widower; his wife had died four years ago. They had had no children and he still lived in the villa he had shared with his wife, which was not far from the city centre.

Emilio called Helena *mia bella ragazza* (my beautiful girl) which reminded her of a Welsh boyfriend she had at university who used to call her his 'lovely girl' in his seductive Welsh accent. For her, this phrase, in whatever language it was spoken, was redolent with ideas not only of love, but of cherishing and protection. Helena needed that and, more than anything, she wanted a man who could say such things without a trace of embarrassment, and mean them. She had found that the Italians she met spoke directly about how they felt, not what they thought. They spoke from the heart. What they felt did not need to be processed by the brain before it was sent out into the world. She didn't care that such utterances might be transient or ephemeral, capable of being changed the very next moment, or that some people might deem them to be lightweight or insincere. For her, they were truthful and honest, spoken without guile. Emilio once said to her, "*La vita ha fatto del tuo viso un bellissimo dipinto*." ("Life has made of your face a most beautiful painting.") She could not think of anyone she had ever met who could have spoken in such a way. It touched her soul.

During her time in Milan, Helena had slowly become herself again. It was as if every step she took on the city's ancient streets and alleyways made her body come alive. Every time she met Emilio, there was always a little gift beside her plate; a bunch of early violets; a slim book of poetry that he had found in a second-hand bookshop. Sometimes, it was an apricot from his garden; a postcard of an illuminated manuscript that she did not know; a simple cotton scarf that he knew would go well with a dress he particularly liked and even, one time, a miniature map of the mountain walk he wanted to take her on. Nothing was expensive or excessive, just thoughtful at the deepest level. She truly was his *bella ragazza*.

Helena and Emilio went walking in the mountains as often as they could. He introduced her to his favourite areas of the Dolomites and they discovered, together, the high pathways of the Alto Adige. The landscape and the views were stunning and they would drive up into the mountains to Bach and after a few days in the rarefied air, come swooping back down the convoluted hairpin bends to the sounds of Boccherini. Sometimes, after a weekend away, he would cook a simple meal for her at his villa. And one evening, he said to her, "Helena, do you want to remain a single woman or would you like to become my wife?" She accepted without hesitation. She needed no one's consent and she certainly did not feel it necessary to ask her children's permission. Indeed, she very rarely heard from them. She phoned them from time to time but they always seemed too busy to chat for long and she guessed that they still felt cheated out of their inheritance. As far as Helena was concerned that was too bad. Over the following weeks, she terminated the lease on her apartment and moved her belongings to Emilio's. She informed the children only that she had moved to a villa and told them nothing of Emilio or her plans. She knew that they would be looking up her address on Google maps as soon as they heard the news. They would, of course, be concerned that she was splashing out and spending 'their' money.

The wedding took place at the city's historic Palazzo Reale in late summer with a small group of friends to wish them well. Later they had a blessing in a medieval chapel in the village of Frapporta in the hills above Lake Garda, where Emilio owned a simple stone house. It was all delightful and perfect. Then, a few weeks after the wedding, she received a phone call from Susan to say that she and Roger were coming over to see her because they wanted to discuss some serious matters. Helena had a sense that it would be something to do with her grandchildren's education. The twins had both muttered from time to time recently about their desire to send their children to good schools, by which, they probably meant somewhere like Marlborough or Charterhouse, and that would mean money, and preferably hers not theirs. She would be ready for them.

They arrived in a taxi one afternoon and had to admit that they were impressed by the villa. Helena greeted them and welcomed them into her home.

"Children, I would like you to meet Emilio. He is my great friend, my lover and my husband." He greeted them courteously as Helena's children. Roger and Susan were shocked and outraged.

"Mother, we have to speak to you," said Roger, pompously.

"I thought that you might, so let us go into the study where we can talk." She closed the door and said, "Before you say one word, I will tell you how things lie. I have made a will and have left your father's inheritance to be divided between your two children. This will be put in trust until they are twenty-one. I will leave you each £5000 and the rest will go to Emilio should he survive me. If not, my remaining estate will go to the Biblioteca Ambrosiana. If you agree to these terms, you are welcome to stay as our guests, which would please us both. If not, there is a perfectly comfortable hotel half a mile away."

Roger asked for a taxi to be called immediately. Helena watched them drive away. "Stone," she thought. "That was the problem. They are stone like their father. I am paper. They are stone." Then she thought of her new surname, Affini; brethren, kindred, affinity. That's what one needed, affinity, and she had found it in Emilio. At last, she felt herself to be among her kin.

Winter Sunrise

Laurence Binyon

It is early morning within this room; without,
Dark and damp; without and within, stillness
Waiting for day; not a sound but a listening air.

Yellow jasmine, delicate on stiff branches,
Stands in a Tuscan pot to delight the eye
In spare December's nakedness.

Suddenly, softly, as if at a breath breathed
On the pale wall, a magical apparition,
The shadow of the jasmine, branch and blossom!

It was not there, it is there, in a perfect image;
And all is changed. It is like a memory lost
Returning without a reason into the mind;

And it seems to me that the beauty of the shadow
Is more beautiful than the flower; a strange beauty,
Pencilled and silently deepening to distinctness.

As a memory stealing out of the mind's slumber,
A memory floating up from dark water,
Can be more beautiful than the thing remembered.